Everything she'd ever done was a horrible sham

Unknowingly, all these years, Stacey had allowed herself to be led into what was already planned for her!

"Damn, *damn!*" she yelled, beginning to sob uncontrollably.

When Hal pulled her into his arms, she clutched at him. "I always thought I was so clever, so smart. And it was all phony. *I'm* a phony!"

"Sssh!" Hal rocked a little from side to side, cradling her. Gradually her sobs turned to sniffs. "Ease up," murmured Hal, tipping her face up. He dropped a light, light kiss on her lips—meant to comfort. A light, light kiss that lingered a moment too long for comfort.

Hal's arms slid to her waist, as if to push her away. "Tell me to get out of here," he growled huskily.

Ann Charlton, Australian author, traces the beginning of her writing to a childhood period when, in trying to avoid nightmares, she began telling herself a story, continued each night. Her professional writing began with a short-story contest. Now, she writes every weekday, interspersed with looking after her family. Tennis, sketching, reading, modern music and dancing are other interests. When both daughters have finished high school, Ann looks forward to travel and seeing new places.

Books by Ann Charlton

HARLEQUIN ROMANCE
2660—A PLACE OF WILD HONEY
2684—NO LAST SONG
2701—WINTER SUN, SUMMER RAIN
2762—THE DRIFTWOOD DRAGON

HARLEQUIN PRESENTS
857—AN IRRESISTIBLE FORCE
912—TITAN'S WOMAN
967—THE DECEPTION TRAP
1008—STREET SONG

Ransomed Heart

Ann Charlton

Harlequin Books

TORONTO • NEW YORK • LONDON
AMSTERDAM • PARIS • SYDNEY • HAMBURG
STOCKHOLM • ATHENS • TOKYO • MILAN

Original hardcover edition published in 1988
by Mills & Boon Limited

ISBN 0-373-02977-2

Harlequin Romance first edition May 1989

CHAPTER ONE

'READ your stars this morning, Stacey?' Alex Warman called as he heard her heels on the garages' cobled forecourt. His birthday was two weeks after hers, which meant he shared Stacey's birth sign, a very fortunate coincidence for Alex, who publicly condemned astrology as a lot of rot, but was able thereby to indulge himself. When he read his stars it was not for himself, but for Stacey. He didn't fool anybody.

'No, but I bet you have,' she said, smiling. Alex was in the corner of the garages known as the House of Stoush, an affectionate name for the old Sydney fight stadium where Alex had briefly enjoyed the limelight as a bantam-weight nearly thirty years ago. There were a few ca-chatter, ca-chatters as he finished working out on the punchball. He emerged wearing the old brown leather boxing-gloves that made his arms look thin and sinewy.

'Let me see—are we expecting a letter from across the sea today?' she mocked. 'Are we to be wise with our spending or——' she rolled her eyes '—is that tall, dark stranger to come into our lives at last, Alex?'

' "Today you take the first step towards a new life," ' quoted Alex, panting a bit from his exertions.

'Is that all? Just as well, I suppose. The tall, dark stranger might have been nice for me, but not a lot of use to you, champ. Done your roadwork yet?' she teased.

Alex was fifty-five, strong and whippy, and kept a

punchball, bag and weights and a battered road bike.

'Did it early,' he said, and cuffed at his nose in the classic fighter's twitch that broke out when he was agitated or excited. 'But not early enough to dodge the headband crowd. Time was when a man could go for a quiet run on his own—now it's fashionable, there's not a safe road about.' He sniffed his disdain for the trendy jogging fraternity.

Stacey put her cameras and accessories bag in her car, then went to help Alex, who was using his teeth to untie one of the gloves. 'Here, let me——' she said, and absently answered a few questions about where she was going and how long she was going to be.

'I have to deliver some black and white negs to Coe's Studios, pick up some darkroom supplies and do a preliminary call about a doggie portrait,' she told him. 'Why is everyone suddenly so nosy about what I'm doing? Anyone would think I was twelve instead of nearly twenty-one!'

Alex looked anxious, nervy. But then, so did everyone else lately. It was Stacey's party. Her parents had arranged a grand affair for her twenty-first, to be held in two weeks in the Jamieson House ballroom. The guest list was as long as the Harbour Bridge, and as studded with Sirs and Hons and hyphens as the Bridge had bolts—a headache for her father, who was very security-conscious. So many prominent guests gathered together constituted a heavy responsibility, and he was almost absurdly concerned about a break-in while the house was filling with the expensive gifts that arrived daily. He'd even talked about hiring some live-in security.

That guest list had been a trial to her mother, too—a nerve-racking exercise in diplomacy, only over-shadowed by the risky business of seating arrangements.

But Clare Jamieson had suspended all worry over the latter when her dress designer had presented her with an unprecedented failure, and she had flown to Melbourne to find the right dress for the night.

If the party was a strain for her mother, every aspect of it was a headache for Alex's wife, Grace. As the housekeeper she had the normal running of the massive house to attend to, in addition to supervising a swarm of casual cleaners and workmen who appeared at intervals.

But Stacey couldn't imagine why Alex should find any of it a strain. When he wasn't chauffeuring her father to and from the office in the Rolls, he worked as a mechanic on the Jamieson cars that were lined up here in a gleaming row—the pale grey Rolls and her father's spare car, a bottle-green Jag, her mother's cream Mercedes and her own silver Alfa sports. Out here, in the relative peace of the garages, Alex should remain untouched by party fever.

'There.' She untied the second glove while she was at it, and left the strings dangling. Bunching her fist, she aimed a mock punch at his chin. 'Bye!'

'A pansy punch—got to keep that wrist up, girl.' Alex cocked an ear as she started her car. 'Don't like the sound of that carburettor.'

'You can take a look at it later, champ.'

Alex winced as she reversed, tyres squealing, on to the forecourt. ' "A day to exercise caution", your stars said,' he called. 'Take it easy on that accelerator. Slow down—no one can keep up with you.'

'Our stars said all that?' Stacey opened her eyes wide at him. 'I hope you'll heed that, Alex, and drive the Rolls with a bit of dignity.'

He snorted. 'You don't think I believe all that mumbo-jumbo, do you?' But he frowned and cuffed at his nose again as she revved the engine. She shot down

the long drive through winter-bare silky oaks and
banked azalea bushes still glistening from the rain
during the night, to join the cypress-lined circular drive.
As usual, Stacey pressed the gate remote control well
before the tall wrought-iron gates came into view
around the cypress pines. Mr Jaswinsky, the gardener,
kept those trees so trimmed, their bulbous shapes so
perfect, that as a child she'd often thought they looked
like cut-outs from the Queen's garden in *Alice in
Wonderland*; almost one-dimensional, overlapping each
other around the white bend of the drive. She pressed
her foot down and the Alfa surged. The drive was one-
way. Incoming cars used the other gates, and whenever
Mr Jaswinsky heard her coming he took his
wheelbarrow and cleared the way. So Stacey was
petrified when she swept around the trees to find a man
outlined against the open gateway. Right in the middle
of the drive, he was, holding a bag in each hand. She
jammed her foot on the brake. The man flung both bags
aside and jack-knifed into a forward roll as the car's
tyres shrieked and skidded. Fine white gravel sprayed up
and ricocheted off the car windows. Then there was
silence, but for the uninterrupted throb of the engine.
For a moment Stacey sat there, open-mouthed, then she
switched off the ignition. She swivelled to look at the
man. He was a body length from the car and sitting up,
quite unharmed, apparently. Stacey leaned out of the
window. 'Whew, that was close! Are you OK?'

There was no answer, but he was on his feet and
looked reasonably agile. 'That was some stunt of
yours,' she said admiringly, able now to appreciate his
quick reflexes and the tight, controlled roll that had
taken him out of the car's path. 'You look as if you've
had training.'

'Stunt?' he repeated, looking over his shoulder at her

as he brushed off his trousers. Stacey eyed him with more interest. What she could see of his face was nothing special, but he was tall and athletic, and there was something about the way he flicked at the dust on his clothes. Her eyes were drawn to his hands—large, powerful hands, restrained and steady. He used the backs of his fingers in small, snappy slaps to his sweater, his jacket. If he was shocked or frightened by the near accident, he had it well in hand.

'I wouldn't have hit you, anyway. I managed to turn the car, as you see.' Stacey waved a hand to indicate the angle of the car skewed across the drive. Then she looked at her watch. 'Well, if you're all right——' She reached for the ignition key and looked down, astounded to find one of his large hands wrapped around her wrist. He leaned through the open window, plucked out the key and tossed it on to the back seat.

'Now, look——' she gasped, awed by the speed and precision of his movements. He opened the door, retaining his grip on her through the window, quickly transferring it when he had her standing. His fingers bit into her upper arm. 'Ow!' she exclaimed.

'Stunt?' he said again, very quietly.

A curious little thrill of warning tingled along Stacey's back. She looked up at him and blinked. A rangy face with a big, straight nose and a big, square chin, craggy cheekbones that crested the long, hollowed slopes of his cheeks. Nothing special, had she thought? He looked like a rough cast by a bold sculptor who had never returned to reduce the proportions—chisel off the chin, refine the bones, trim that thrusting nose. But then he would have looked like a hundred other good-looking men. Like this, he *was* something special. That mouth—asymmetrical, tilted sadly on one side, dented angrily into his cheek on the other. And those eyes—

hard to tell about the eyes. They were narrowed right down and could have been any colour at all. At her prolonged inspection they narrowed still more. He gave her the suggestion of a shake.

'That was not a stunt, Miss Jamieson—I imagine I'm right in assuming you're the Jamieson brat?'

Stacey's eyes opened wide at that. He went on before she could open her mouth as well.

'Your admiration is gratifying, but I am not in the habit of performing circus tricks in people's driveways. That "stunt" was to save my life because *you* were driving like a maniac.'

'I never drive like a maniac!' she protested. 'I'm an excellent driver. It's your fault!'

The indented side of his mouth indented further. 'Well, of course it's my fault. I will go hurling myself at speeding sports cars. It's a lucky thing I didn't damage your car.'

Loftily, she ignored his sarcasm. 'The drive is one-way——' She inclined her head towards the semicir-cular drive. 'Incoming traffic uses the gate down there—outgoing here. You came in the wrong gate. Incidentally, you're supposed to use the intercom and give your name, not just nip in when the gates happen to open. What are you doing here?' She eyed the flung bags. 'If you're selling something——'

His hands tightened around her arms and Stacey felt herself nearly lifted off the ground. Brown eyes—the deep brown eyes you'd expect with black hair, rather than his mid-brown.

'No, I am not selling something. As from today I'm working here, God help me. I should have taken extra insurance!'

Working here? Extra staff arrived every day to prepare the house for the party. None like this one, though. None with muscles nor manners like his. Speakingly, Stacey twitched one arm against his punishing grip. 'Let me guess,' she drawled. 'You've come to help out with the floral arrangements.'

He gave a snort of laughter; her quip had, it seemed, got past his guard. 'Hal Stevens,' he said. 'Security.'

'Oh.' That explained the bags. Her father had said someone was coming to live in at the house until the party, but she'd assumed he would be the kind of security man who ghosted around the place from time to time when her father felt particularly threatened —pleasant men of indeterminate age and feature. Big men often, but running to seed.

'You don't look the usual type. You're more——'

His mouth hardened. 'More what?'

Stacey ran her eyes over his impressive shoulders and deep chest. She grinned. 'Just—more.'

His hands dropped away from her. He tipped his head back a fraction and looked down his nose at her. Eyes as cold as ice—no, brown eyes couldn't look cold as ice. Cold as marble? Cold as cold black coffee?

'No apology, Miss Jamieson? Not even a simple "I'm sorry" for nearly blowing me to kingdom come? Not even an enquiry as to whether my clothes were damaged?'

'Were they? Let me see.' She nudged his arm and, surprised, he took a half-step so that she could see the back of his jacket. It was a robust, tweedy fabric and none the worse for wear. It looked great on him. Or rather, he looked great in it. Stepping in front of him, Stacey took the lapels in both hands and held the jacket open. 'Yes, you've pulled some threads on your sweater,' she nodded. 'Just let our housekeeper know how much it cost and she'll reimburse you——'

Hal Stevens took her wrists, and removed her hands

from his clothes. 'You're a callous little bitch, aren't you?' he said conversationally. Stacey gaped, drawing herself up to rebuke him for that, but he just held her gaze, and somehow she couldn't think of anything to say that would be likely to put down a man with such a flinty look in his eye. In fact, his whole face looked carved and flinty, the high spots and hollows sharply etched in sunlight and shadow. She could almost see him through a viewfinder—three-quarter profile, side-lit—and it utterly distracted her.

'Would you let me photograph you?' she asked earnestly.

He tipped his head sideways, as if he'd heard wrong. *'What?'* he demanded.

'I'd like to take some pictures of you. You have an interesting facial structure.' She pointed to his cheek. 'This hollow here is terrific, and you have that grainy sort of skin that would photograph so well in black and white——' Lightly, she touched his cheekbone, drawing her finger down to his jaw, and at once her professional detachment vanished. Her fingertip tingled as if she'd received a low-voltage charge. Once again he caught her wrist and held it poised, looking at her in disbelief. He gave a dry laugh, as if he was reluctant to let go of his anger to be amused. 'No, I will *not* let you photograph me.'

The tingling feeling persisted. She hadn't meant to touch him like that; it wasn't her style to stroke the faces of strangers, but she hadn't been able to resist it. It shook her a bit. 'I'd give you some free prints, of course. For your girlfriend—or your wife, if you're married. Are you?'

Levelly, Hal Stevens held her gaze. Without answering, he turned and picked up his bags. Stacey had never seen any reason to be coy about asking what she wanted to know, and people usually told her. Suddenly, though, she wished she hadn't asked that question. Carrying the bags, he came towards her again. He limped slightly this time. Was he hurt, after all? Frowning, Stacey tried to recall any sign of a limp before this. There had been none. She concentrated on it as he walked past her, as she was obviously meant to do. 'Oh, yes!' she said admiringly, 'that's very good—the old soldier limp. It came on suddenly. Am I supposed to be stricken with conscience and offer you a million dollars in compensation?'

Hal Stevens looked back. He took a deep breath. 'Sweetheart, you might be able to do the second, but I doubt very much if you've ever been stricken with anything, including conscience.'

'Oh, that's a bit harsh,' she said flippantly to hide the fact that his words and that scornful glance hurt her in some way. It was ridiculous! He just worked for her father. He was nobody. Why should she care if he didn't like her?

As Stevens walked along the drive, Alex appeared and looked him over. With his boxer's eye, he'd probably already established the man's excellent physical condition, even allotted him a fighting weight. He could do it at a glance. Stacey slipped behind the wheel of the Alfa, and reversed until she was level with the two men. Stevens eyed the car the way a hunter might eye a wounded elephant. Through the window she said, 'Looks like our tall, dark stranger finally turned up, Alex. Meet Hal Stevens.' She met the new man's eyes mockingly. 'He's come to help with the flower arrangements.'

Alex looked taken aback at that, and she thought, but couldn't be sure as she drove away, that Hal Stevens smiled.

That evening she dressed for a date and, with only her ear-rings to be fixed, went downstairs to the library where her father always drank a whisky sour and smoked a cigar on his return from the office. He was by the window, his substantial body outlined against the faded plum-covered velvet curtains. This was a room that appeared to have escaped her mother's perennial re-decorating. It was a traditional gentleman's retreat with its Turkish rugs and leather wing-backed chairs, old books and a display case full of Victorian treasures—a stuffed owl, butterflies, silver-mounted emu and ostrich eggs. It looked like a room that had been occupied by consecutive heirs—a room where Great-grandfather had sat, and Grandfather. But it was an illusion. Her own great-grandfather had been an undistinguished cabinet-maker, and her grandfather a tailor. All these furnishings had come from genuine rooms like this, the leather chairs worn and shined by genuine aristocratic rears, the intrepid Victorian explorer's collection bought from the estate of an intrepid Victorian explorer. This room, so shabbily genteel, so ancestral, was in fact a tribute to her monther's decorating genius.

Her father turned and saw her, his frown lifting.

'Hello, pet,' he said. Stacey went over and kissed his cheek. Was it her imagination, or did he look rather drawn? Hard to tell. He was a big man who tried to forget that in his youth he'd driven his own trucks and repaired them and dug them out of mud. The early days, before he'd made enough money to discover his own financial genius. But that phase of his life was etched in his hard strength, a largeness of gesture and an indefinable toughness that lingered in speech and posture, no matter how hard he tried to temper it or disguise it with English tailoring and fine linen and manicures. Brian Jamieson had the indestructibility of a man who had done things the hard way and won. Stacey couldn't think why this party he insisted on throwing for her should have him so rattled. Of course, he might have business worries. He'd built Talisman from the ground up, and still worked long hours as chairman. He hadn't taken a holiday in years. Over fifty, overweight, overworked—a prime candidate for a heart attack, Stacey often worried.

'You're working too hard,' she said, and rubbed a forefinger across the crease on his forehead, smoothing it out. 'When did you last have a check-up?'

'What kind of a greeting is that?' her father complained. 'I'm fine—fine.'

'You know Dr Dalkeith told you to slow down or lose some weight.' She eyed his drink and his cigar. 'And give up a few little indulgences.'

'Doctors! Only ever tell you to give up what you like. I'd have a lot more time for the profession if one of them advised me to give up shaving or muesli or opera for the sake of my health.' He lowered his voice on 'opera', cast a scared look at the door in case Clare should hear. All an act. Brian Jamieson did what he wanted in his own home and everywhere else. He loathed opera, but did not let that stand in the way of social necessity. Unlike Clare, who had had a classical musical education and was a fair pianist, he had grown up knowing little about music and nothing of opera. But with his usual efficiency he had applied himself to finding out. Now he was quite expert on the subject. He and Clare were Friends of the Opera and went to all the first nights and parties, where he discussed it with becoming seriousness.

Stacey laughed. 'You hypocrite, Dad!'

'Pragmatist, pet. You'll find a lot of them in opera

audiences,' he said drily. 'Now, where's Chris taking you tonight?'

'The theatre. A new Williamson play.' She clamped an envelope bag under one arm, and grappled with an ear-ring and an earlobe. Her father's attention homed in on the ear-ring as she slotted it in. It was a pretty green and gold hoop that matched the silk-knit sweater she wore over cream trousers.

'The theatre?' He inspected her clothes. 'Dressed like that—with plastic ear-rings?'

'It's not a first night, Dad, and hardly anyone gets their evening gowns out for the theatre any more. And it's costume jewellery—but I don't think it's plastic.'

'Hmph,' said her father. Jewellery was the real stuff, or not at all. He set his cigar in an ashtray on his massive pedestal desk, and unlocked one of the mahogany drawers.

'But never mind about my ear-rings. Tell me about this security man you've hired. Hal something or other——' Stacey remembered the name perfectly well, but felt impelled to pretend otherwise. 'Oh, darn it!' She dropped the other ear-ring, and it skittered across the Turkish rug. She crouched down, but couldn't see it. 'He came on like something out of a Bond movie today.' She lowered her face to the ground and peered under a chesterfield. Somewhere beyond its bulk her father said something, but she couldn't hear. Crawling forward, eyes scanning left and right for a green and gold ear-ring, she rounded one of the wing-back chairs and raised her voice. 'Is he married?'

There was a foot planted in front of the wing-back chair. Two feet, in brown leather. Stacey gaped at them, then raised her eyes. A hand appeared, a green and gold ear-ring held between finger and forefinger. She raised her eyes some more, and a face leaned towards her, brown eyes mocking. 'The name is Stevens,' Hal Stevens said softly. 'And no, he's not.'

For the second time that day Stacey wished she hadn't asked the question. The man would think she was obsessed with his marital status, and she wasn't—only curious, that was all. He looked amused, as no doubt he was, with her crouched like an Indian scout on all fours at his feet. Glaring, she snatched the ear-ring and scrambled to her feet, shaking off his offered assistance.

'Heavens, I didn't know you were there, Mr Stevens,' she said lightly. 'But I suppose being sneaky is the hallmark of a good security operative.'

'No, Miss Jamieson—it's being fast on your feet.'

Ignoring the double-edged reply, she took another stab at getting the ear-ring in. Hal Stevens was smoking a cigar, too. The chair's lavish proportions had hidden him, but she should have seen the smoke. No smoke without fire. He held the fat Havana between his index finger and thumb—hoodlum fashion. He could look a real thug, what with his big muscles and harsh-boned face—a real hard man. But there was an indefinable air about him that saved him from it. His hair was thick and classily cut, and he had exchanged his sweater and tweedy jacket for a soft rust shirt and blazer. But that was only window-dressing. Whatever it was about him came from some inner confidence or strength. 'What security firm do you work for, Mr Stevens?' she asked. 'Are you from Talisman?'

'Hal was in the police force for a time, and he used to work for me in security at Talisman,' her father put in dismissively, closing and locking his desk drawer. 'But he has his own business nowadays.'

'What kind of business?' asked Stacey, eyes on the man. For a security man, he made her feel amazingly insecure. 'Will you depend on brain or brawn to protect us from intruders, Mr Stevens?'

Goadingly, he made her wait while he exhaled cigar smoke.

'My partner and I run a martial arts academy,' he said.

'Ah!' Stacey smiled. Brawn, not brain. She didn't have to say it out loud; disappointingly, he seemed only amused at the intended slight.

Her father took her hand and firmly set a small box in it. 'Something I was saving for you,' he said. 'Wear them tonight, pet.'

They were ear-rings—fine gold, set with diamonds.

'They're beautiful, Dad!' She kissed his cheek. 'But too much with this outfit——'

'To please me,' said her father, an arm bracingly around her. He took the green and gold piece from her hand and replaced it with a diamond ear-ring plucked from the box with his big, blunt fingers. 'I don't want my daughter going around in bits of plastic. Come on, wear them, to please your old Dad,' he said, squeezing her shoulders, and she sighed.

'Oh, all right.' Removing the other fake ear-ring, she fitted a diamond one to her lobe, conscious of Hal Stevens watching. A few times she glanced at him, wondering what he was thinking. Stacey had no illusions about her looks, nor any false modesty. She might not be dressed formally tonight as her father would have liked, but she knew she looked good. Green was a colour that suited her, bringing out the green bias in her blue-green eyes, making her fox-brown hair redder—or 'foxier', as her hairdresser would say. Ramón frequently added 'foxy' highlights to her hair. It was an eye-catching feature, past shoulder-length, thick and carefully layered and waved to look as if she stood permanently in a light, flattering breeze. Her colouring was her greatest asset, and perhaps her mouth, which was wide but proportionately full as well, but because of her hair men were often misled into believing her a beauty. Hal Stevens' eyes followed the sway of it as she flicked her head. She would be very surprised if he was misled. The man made her uneasy, and it wasn't only because they'd met in less than amiable circumstances. There was something in his expression that reminded her of something or someone, and she didn't like it. Now she wished she had resisted her father's urgings to wear his gift. Under Hal Stevens' scrutiny she was beginning to feel like a store mannequin being decked out.

Chris's car drew up in the front drive, cutting short her father's indulgent approval. Stacey was uncharacteristically anxious to be gone. Even when Brian Jamieson picked up the discarded costume jewellery and threw it into his waste bin, she stayed only long enough to protest, and not to rescue it.

'I'll be home at about one, I expect, Mr Stevens,' she said, forcing herself to meet that disturbing gaze. 'You won't mistake me for a burglar and fell me with a karate chop now, will you?'

It was twelve-thirty, in fact, when Stacey arrived home. She was half expecting to see the security man lurking about. She was half glad he wasn't—half disappointed. Disgruntled with her inconsistency, she became critical of his non-appearance. So much for his vigilance! She could be a burglar and make off with all her birthday presents while he no doubt slept like a baby in one of the guest-rooms. Stacey smiled. She really must point that out when she saw him at breakfast.

But she saw him a lot sooner than that.

CHAPTER TWO

IT SEEMED she had hardly closed her eyes before she woke again. Stacey stared up at the tester of her four-poster bed, trying to snatch at the surrealist shreds of a dream. She dreamed a lot lately. With a sigh, she threw back the covers. She was hot and had a raging thirst. She should never touch red wine, she thought. Unfortunately, Chris believed that red was the only real wine, and white just lolly-water. Stacey got out of bed, turned down the heater thermostat and drank the glass of water by her bed. Then she dragged off her long-sleeved night-gown and tossed it on the floor. Yawning, she rummaged through some drawers to find something cooler. It was hit or miss by moonlight, but she couldn't be bothered with lights. In the end, half the drawers' contents were on the floor, and she plucked out a wisp of summery black lace.

Naked, she spread out her arms, pirouetting to cool her skin, and ended up by the glass case that gleamed in the moonlight from her windows. The black nightdress draped behind her on the floor as she leaned on the cool glass, gazing at her collection of seashells. Twice a year during her redecorating raids, her mother tried to talk her into getting rid of the shells, or at least relegating them to the cellar. But Stacey didn't care whether they complemented the curtains or the rugs or the wallpapers, and she stubbornly refused to let them go. Resting her chin on the glass, she looked with pleasure at the striped, curled, spiked and whirled shapes. The moonlight silvered their delicate pinks and mauves, the translucency of burnished mother-of-pearl.

As a child she had found them buried in the sand or gleaming in rock pools, her excitement at the discovery of yet another beautiful shell exceeded only by the delicious sense of achievement.

'I found it all by myself!' she would boast to envious friends who found only periwinkles and pippi-shells which anyone could find. She had taken her collection to school, and even the unimpressible Miss Markham had been impressed, though she had given Stacey a funny, adult look of indulgence when she said she had found them all by herself. 'They're my jewels, Miss Markham,' she'd said, for that was what she called them in the days before she learned that the real jewels were her mother's diamonds and sapphires and emeralds. Stacey smiled, and pressed a fingertip against a delicate burst of spikes.

The shells were reminders of childhood and magic and fantasy, days of sunshine. She picked up a glossy golden cowrie and rubbed it absently against her cheek. Always sunshine. But it must have rained sometimes, surely, during all those holidays spent at one or another of their beach houses. Stacey could recall no rain, only the sun which prompted her mother or Nanny Driesfeld to coat her nose with cream and coax her to stay in the shade of the beach umbrella.

She returned the shell to its glass shelf. It was a bit childish, she supposed, holding on to these. 'But it's not as if I take a teddy bear to bed,' she told herself, as if defending herself against accusations of babyish behaviour. The black lace went over her head. She stretched her arms up and gave a little shimmy to encourage the nightshift down. It had barely reached her waist when she saw the shadow that shouldn't be there. Arms still raised, Stacey went rigid. It was a human-shaped shadow—a large, man-shaped shadow beside the northernmost french doors and their looped-back curtains. It was a relaxed shadow leaning on the wall, just waiting. Waiting.

Her mouth opened wide and the shadow took solid form, lunged from the wall and was on her, one hand smothering her scream, the other twisting her around so that her assailant was behind her.

'Relax,' he said. 'It's me.'

Stacey recognised the voice, but it was not the relief he seemed to expect it to be. She kicked and couldn't make contact, she grabbed the spikiest shell from the glass case and lashed out with it, but he spun her around, pressed her face against him so that her yells were muffled. Then he took her weapon from her with humiliating ease. 'It's me—Stevens. Calm down!'

Stacey took a huge breath to scream, but her nose was flattened into his shoulder, and she got precious little air into her lungs, and all of it smelling of him. Cautiously he eased her away, and her head fell back as she gasped for air. A scream was out of the question, but she managed a breathless, 'Get your hands off me!' That was top priority, getting rid of those large, controlled hands that had so fascinated her. They were half-on, half-off the nightdress which had bunched around her waist and stayed there.

'Keep your voice down,' he told her, calm as you please. His face was partly shadowed, but she caught a glint of moonlight in his eyes. He looked fearsome, carved out of rock.

'Keep my voice down?' she repeated, trying desperately for some volume. 'Calm down? Relax? Are you mad? You dare come in here and touch me——' Eyes widening, she realised then that he must have been here all the time, must have seen her strip off. Her skin took fire. 'Voyeur!' she snapped, then opened her mouth wide again, but a massive hand plastered itself over the lower half of her face. Furiously she glared at him over it.

'Could you abuse me quietly?' he asked, as if it was a perfectly reasonable request. He lowered his hand a fraction.

'Pervert!' she yelped. The hand went back.

'It isn't what you might think, Miss Jamieson. Please be quiet. Your father is already very uptight about security, as I'm sure you know. A screech from you at two in the morning might give him a heart attack.'

She went still at that, but after a second or two began to struggle, her yells reduced to impotent mumbles as her mouth opened and shut against the warm palm of his hand.

'I'm not here to slake my passions, so put any Gothic notions of the kind out of your mind. You may very well be irresistible to men who can afford you, but you don't do a thing for me.' Stacey wrestled against his grasp. Frantically she tried to pull the nightshift down past her waist. Even more frantically she tried to hold her bare lower body away from him. It didn't appease her at all when he tried to assist her, using one hand. 'Don't touch me——' Tears of frustration and humiliation burned on her eyelids. God, he'd seen everything!

His voice went on, low and unemotional. 'I was doing my rounds and found your terrace doors unlocked. Through the glass I saw that you hadn't activated your alarm, so I came in to do it. If you hadn't woken, I would have left via the internal door and you none the wiser, that's all. Got it?'

He let her go, and she could think of nothing but

being covered. The black lace came down at last, too late, and she snatched up a dressing-gown and dragged it around her. 'Activate my alarm?' she spat, rounding on him. He'd done that all right! 'That's a weak excuse to come sneaking in here, scaring me half to death. You're over-zealous, Stevens. When my father hears about this——'

'Tch, tch! Going to tell tales to Daddy?' he mocked.

'This isn't part of your job. No burglars are going to come in via this room, right at the front of the house. Why don't you go check the back rooms, and keep your fancy holds for your martial arts school, or the women who *like* the macho bandit-in-the-night stuff——'

'Oh, pipe down,' he said, and went to the french doors where first she'd seen him. He reached up and pressed a button, and the tiny red light came on. She must have woken up before he could activate it. His story certainly seemed credible, but it didn't mollify her one bit.

'I'm sorry you've been disturbed,' he said, as if she had suffered no more than the merest inconvenience. And, before she could really cut loose on him, he was gone.

In the morning, as had been her habit over the past week, Stacey went to the small sitting-room where her birthday gifts were piling up. She lined up the latest three to have arrived and, tucking her robe about her, sat cross-legged on the carpet to study them. Her concentration wasn't good on this occasion. She kept thinking about the Stevens man. To drive out the images that brought, she said doggedly, 'Mr and Mrs Fitzroy-Majors, thank you for——' She stopped, looked at the leather-bound book which was the Fitzroy-Majors' gift to her, a first edition of a fairly obscure account of the Colony of New South Wales. 'What rhymes with

Fitzroy-Majors?' she sighed, and left the antique book for a moment, moving on to a Fabergé egg, the gift of Dr and Mrs Dalkeith. Dr Dalkeith was the one who had given her father the advice he disliked and ignored. He had very large front teeth. Stacey grinned at the beautiful jewelled egg. 'Doc Dalkeith, you're a honey—for making like the Easter bunny.' Pleased, she nodded, adding a Bugs Bunny chomp. 'Eh—what's up, Doc?'

Something alerted her, and she turned to see Hal Stevens leaning in the doorway. The pose appeared to be typical of the man. It was how he had stood in her room last night while she had cavorted about naked and draped herself over the glass case, gawping and grinning like a kid at her shells, babbling about taking teddy bears to bed. Her face darkened. Now he'd caught her imitating a cartoon rabbit! She shouldn't be surprised to see him, after all, he had been hired to keep an eye on the valuables, but her heart-rate accelerated as if she'd been startled by a burglar.

'Good morning,' he said. He looked uncertain, and for a moment Stacey thought he might have realised he'd put his job in jeopardy by manhandling the boss's daughter last night, but she dismissed the idea. Stevens didn't seem the man to let a little thing like that bother him. As his gaze wandered around, then settled on her—cross-legged on the floor with a book, a jewelled egg and a pair of Victorian lustres lined up before her, she decided he was just plain puzzled. She wished now that she'd dressed before she came in here, and flipped the end of her robe over her bare feet. A habit of hers, that, forgetting to put anything on her feet. Her face warmed. It was almost coy, tucking her toes out of sight when he'd had the grand tour. 'Is there *nothing* I can do without you spying on me, Mr Stevens?' she demanded.

'I'm here to protect the goods,' he reminded her,

with a short gesture at the gifts laid out on tables. There was speculation in his eyes—not the colour of cold black coffee this morning, but hot coffee with a dash of milk. Stacey turned back to her task, wishing she'd brushed her hair, but resisting the reflex to tidy it. It struck her that she was always wishing to change something when he was about. Somehow, she was never quite ready for him.

'May I ask what you're doing?' He came in to prop himself on the corner of one of the tables, which meant his long legs were stretched out beside her. She found it distracting.

'I have to memorise who gives me what,' she said shortly. 'At the party I'll be greeting the guests, and I have to be able to remember what everyone gave me and talk about it——'

His mouth thrust out thoughtfully. 'Didn't Brian say there were over three hundred guests?'

'Three hundred and fifty-six at the last count. That's only about a hundred and seventy-five presents, of course.'

'Only?' he said drily. '*Will* you remember them all?'

Stacey looked up at him. He'd been here less than twenty-four hours, and this was the second time she'd been at his feet. 'Of course. I use rhymes to fix them in my memory——'

He looked at the Fabergé egg, then slowly grinned. 'Ah—that explains the Easter bunny. What have you got for the book?' He seemed quite interested. There was a spark of something in his eyes she hadn't seen before. Such deep brown eyes. Moroccan coffee with cream, she amended the colour. But she didn't care that much for coffee. 'Nothing yet. Unless you have a rhyme for Fitzroy-Majors?'

He grimaced. 'A tough one. What are those?' He pointed to the delicate candlesticks with their mini-chandelier fringes of cut crystal.

'Lustres,' she sighed. 'Given to me by Sir Henry and Lady Sedgwick. If only people would give me furs and rings and gold!'

His mouth twisted as he surveyed the exquisite paintings, perfume, crystal, silver. 'That's what you'd prefer?'

Stacey got up. 'No. I hate furs and I hardly ever wear rings. Gold's OK. They'd be easy to rhyme, that's all. Sedgwick and lustres have their limitations.'

His rich chuckle surprised her—him too, apparently, for he sobered, regarded her almost warily. Stacey felt wary herself, and was annoyed to discover her hands fussing around, overlapping her robe edges, tightening her belt. 'You don't do a thing for me,' he'd said. She'd tried to forget he said that because, really, it didn't matter a damn. But it rankled.

'I could have you fired because of last night,' she told him, fixing him with an icy look. He blinked at the sudden change.

'And will you?' he enquired, as she passed him on her way to the door.

'I don't know yet.' She looked back at him haughtily. 'If you come up with a rhyme for Fitzroy-Majors, you might be worth keeping on.' The deliberate hint of patronage in her tone didn't bother him. He just smiled as if he was above any moves she might make, and walked alongside her. Presumably he was going back to his room to shave before breakfast. The man's jaw was stubbled. Stacey's fingers itched, whether to touch the sandpapery texture or whether to grab a camera to photograph it, she wasn't entirely sure. As they passed the bedroom next to the gifts, which she assumed was his room, she looked at him, puzzled. She looked at him again when he was still beside her at her own door. Dismayed, she watched him walk along to enter the suite next to hers. At his door he glanced back at her, and gave a mocking little nod before he went in.

Jamieson House was a mansion featured frequently in magazines for its grand, cantilevered staircase, upstairs arched gallery and a marble-floored, chandeliered entrance salon. It had a ballroom, also much photographed for the coffered ceiling installed before the turn of the century; it had an enormous kitchen and a breakfast-room, dining-rooms, three drawing-rooms and the library. It had a tennis court and pool and a conservatory, semi-detached servants' quarters, now the Warmans' flat; it had a full-sized cellar and a flower-room, lounges, eight bedrooms and six bathrooms. With all this space to spare, Stacey saw no reason why Hal Stevens should occupy the bedroom suite next to hers.

But her objections on the matter were dismissed summarily by her father, and in front of Stevens, too. He'd beaten her down to breakfast and already given a report on the matter of her failure to set her alarm, but not, Stacey bet, on the matter of his voyeurism. If he had admitted to that, her father might be less single-minded about her alarm.

'Stacey, I must *insist* that you lock your doors and set your alarm every night without fail. If you don't, Hal has my permission to go in and do it——'

She gaped, unbelieving that her father would override her sovereignty in her own bedroom and allow a stranger such familiarity. It was on the tip of her tongue to tell him that this trusted employee had handled her while she was half dressed, but one glance at Hal Stevens changed her mind. 'In that case,' she said frigidly, 'my alarm will be set day and night.'

Her father patted her hand. 'Good girl! Now what are you doing today, pet? Lunching with Chris? Another fitting for your party dress?'

Stevens' mouth twisted a bit, and she squirmed. It was the sort of thing her father always said, but with the security man watching it sounded trivial. She wished he'd asked about her charity work or her current photo commissions instead. There she went again—wanting to change something just because Hal Stevens was there. Brian Jamieson gathered up his financial papers to leave for the office. Stevens spread some of Grace's cumquat marmalade on toast, and poured himself some coffee. Stacey brought up the subject of Hal's room, pointing out that even with his speed and sneakiness he might not make it along the gallery to the gifts in case of a burglary, and surely he would be more suitably accommodated in the small guest bedroom? Her father cleared his throat as if he was at a board meeting, told her to enjoy herself and let them worry about things like that. 'Your presents are in Hal's safe hands, pet.' He kissed her and left, cutting short any further discussion.

Stacey stared at Hal Stevens' 'safe' hands, which were busy buttering more toast, pouring more coffee. She really didn't want him using the bedroom right next to hers. There was no defined reason for it. Then again, there was no real reason why he *should* be there. It was a superior guest suite, and he wasn't a guest, he was an employee. Let him sleep somewhere else. She glared at his downturned head and, as if he sensed her watching, he looked up. For a moment he held her gaze.

'How about—"Thank you, Mrs Fitzroy-Majors, for the bunch of history pages"?' he said.

Stacey blinked—and, in spite of everything, laughed. 'That's terrible!'

'It rhymes,' he pointed out, taking a bite of toast.

Stacey murmured the rhyme to herself a few times.

'It's terrible, but I like it.' Again that small, mocking nod. She got up and went to the door. 'I could still have you fired.'

'I'll try to learn to live with the uncertainty,' he assured her.

She smiled as she went upstairs. It was to be hoped that he kept his sense of humour, because she was going to move him out of his luxury suite into something more suitable. Something considerably more distant from her own room. First, though, she had to sell the idea to Grace Warman, who ruled supreme over the accommodation arrangements. It wouldn't be easy, for Grace had already made up her mind that she liked Hal. He was lucky. On the rare occasions when Grace didn't 'take' to house guests, certain chemical and physical laws were put into motion. One of her meals could smile at a favoured recipient and, with some mysterious alteration governed entirely by Grace's mood, lie there reluctantly for the unfavoured. Judging by the relish with which he'd finished his breakfast, Mr Stevens had been awarded the meal of approval.

'But your father said he was to have that suite,' said Grace when Stacey broached the subject in the kitchen. Grace was kneading bread dough at the big, bleached pine table. Slap, slap, fold and turn. Stacey drank some fruit juice while she watched the ritual that always preceded the most delectable dinner rolls. Grace's bread was legendary. So was her self-discipline. She cooked pastries and gourmet meals, but was a strict vegetarian herself—tall and youthfully dark-haired. Amazing Grace, Stacey called her.

'He must have made a mistake, Grace. I mean, does it seem right to you? A man sleeping in the room next to me?'

Grace looked askance at her. 'Got a touch of the pruderies all of a sudden, have we?' she said drily.

'No, but I'd—really feel better if he—slept somewhere

else.' Stacey let her eyes slide away, and Grace stopped her kneading.

'He's not a toucher, is he?' A toucher was that lowest of low creatures in Grace's book. Years ago, an unfortunate toucher had chosen Grace's behind as his target, and she had floored him in a crowded Melbourne tram.

'Now I didn't say that,' Stacey disclaimed with the air of one who doesn't wish to ruin a man's entire reputation. Grace read between the lines.

'My hat! I wouldn't have thought he was the type. But then that's the trouble, isn't it? They never are,' she added with dubious logic. She dealt the dough a couple of punches that Alex could have used in his last fight. 'You're sure now?'

'Well, I wouldn't like to jump to conclusions,' Stacey said mendaciously. 'He might just have been doing his job, as he claims, but he was in my room at two this morning——'

Wham! The dinner rolls took a final blow and were out for the count. Stacey regretfully eyed the dough, which already wore a mutinous look. No fluffy dinner rolls today. Still, it was a small price to pay, she thought, as she took herself off with Grace's blessing and her bunch of spare keys, to move Hal Stevens to more suitable lodgings. She took the precaution of checking first on his whereabouts. Stacey had no intention of tangling with him about it—she wanted to present him with a *fait accompli*.

Eventually she tracked him down in Alex's House of Stoush. The leather punchball was ca-chatter, ca-chattering as Hal Stevens worked out on it almost lazily, using one fist, then the other.

'He's a very handy light heavyweight,' Alex told her with the air of a trainer with his protégé, while Hal continued his rhythmic exercise. 'His dad was at my last fight, you know.' Alex looked a bit sorrowful at that. He had lost on a knockout that last fight, and it was his everlasting shame that he hadn't retired on his feet. Even thirty years later, he would like to go back for that one last punch to put things right. Hal moved to the canvas punchbag. He wore a sleeveless black sweatshirt, and his bare arms bulged with muscle, glistened with perspiration. The heavy action rippled through his shoulders and chest. The man was in remarkable shape—big, strong but not too heavy. An athlete. He looked around suddenly and met Stacey's eyes across the clutter of Alex's tyre black and upholstery shampoo, and she felt uncomfortably like a voyeur. And that reminded her of last night, which in turn reminded her of the task in hand. Now that she knew he was nicely tied up here for a while, she could move his gear out.

She would never make it as a criminal, she thought ten minutes later, in his room. This was her home, yet the adrenalin pumped through her body as if she was a housebreaker. It seemed a simple thing; pack up his stuff and have it moved to another room. Maids did it all the time. Stacey stalled. For one thing, touching his personal possessions was amazingly intimate. For another, although she reminded herself of his intrusion into her room last night, she felt guilty. She moved about the room, picking up a blue towelling robe, pyjama bottoms but no top. So he was all macho and bare-chested in bed, was he? Stacey didn't let the image develop. She retrieved a hand-knitted blue sweater which lay over a chair. Who knitted him sweaters? she wondered, handling it gingerly. Oh, this was awful! Some burglars, she'd read, actually got a kick out of handling other people's belongings. It didn't work for her. No way was she going to be able to go through Hal Stevens' drawers and wardrobe. Stacey had decided to forget the whole thing and give the task to Grace, when the door opened.

Hal Stevens stood there for a moment. His eyes narrowed on her, then flicked around the room. He stepped inside and closed the door to lean back on it. The move made Stacey feel as if every avenue for escape had been cut off. He was still dressed in the sleeveless sweat-shirt and track-suit pants, and had a small towel slung around his neck. With his bare arms crossed and his long, muscular body on a relaxed incline, he looked infinitely more dangerous than he had with the gloves on. Stacey clutched the armful of clothes defensively.

Hal Stevens strolled into the room. 'An unexpected pleasure,' he said softly, glancing over the paperbacks and clipboard notes beside the bed, the bunch of keys dangling from her hand. Casually he tried the bureau, which was locked. 'But you should have checked with me first. I like my privacy. But perhaps you don't feel mere employees are entitled to that, Miss Jamieson?'

Stacey's self-disgust and guilt vanished. 'Privacy?' she echoed. 'You talk about privacy when you had the gall to—to skulk around my room last night?'

'It's my job to skulk,' he said sardonically.

'Job or not, my bedroom is off limits to you. If you enter it again I'll see to it you're sacked—and believe me, it won't do your reputation any good to be sacked by a Jamieson if you want any more jobs like this.'

'Jobs like this! Do I look like a masochist?' he snorted. 'Babysitting a spoiled, over-protected little—brat's birthday baubles isn't my idea of fulfilling work. I'm doing this as a favour to your father.'

'Well, do yourself a favour and stay out of my room!' She headed for the door, but he got there before her, leaning one arm on the wall, barring her way. He used the towel to dab away moisture on his neck and forehead. His hair was thick and tough-looking, yet all around his hairline the short, damp ends had curled into fine, wispy baby curls. The incongruity distracted her. The towel dropped back over his shoulders. Softly, he spoke. 'It's not my fault, you know, that I saw you without your clothes.' Her colour went sky-high. 'When you woke, I just kept quiet figuring you'd go back to sleep and I'd let myself out without frightening you.' There was humour in his eyes. 'I couldn't know that you'd get up and play with your toys and perform a striptease at two in the morning, now could I?'

'But I'll bet you watched!' she accused. 'I'll bet you didn't close your eyes!'

Laughter tugged at his mouth, squeezing up the corners of his eyes as they roamed over her furious face. 'A good security man never closes his eyes,' he murmured.

'You——' Her voice choked in her throat. If he wasn't so big and so sweaty she would hit him! Hal Stevens sobered.

'However, the light was poor, and a good security man also has a selective memory. What little I saw is already forgotten, Miss Jamieson.'

The professional, almost courtly attempt to mollify her only inflamed her more. 'Don't give me that, you—you pervert!'

There was a noticeable hardening of his expression. His face was not unlike one of those Easter Island statues when he looked like this—calm but implacable. Enigmatic. He really would make a superb subject. Stacey tried to push past him, but came up against him with a jolt. Her hand spread on his chest. He was warm and damp and very substantial, and nothing like a statue to touch. The smell of the man was musky, acutely masculine —and already familiar. 'Get out of my way!' she commanded, alarmed by that. But he didn't move.

'I suppose you have some reason for nosing around here, Miss Jamieson,' he said, 'but I confess I'm baffled.

Women don't usually come uninvited to my room to play with my clothes.' He looked at the garments she clutched to her breast. Raising his eyes mockingly to hers, he added, 'Not unless I'm wearing them.'

She thrust the clothes at him. 'Maybe we should have accommodated you in the ballroom, Mr Stevens,' she said, acid-sweet. 'You must be pushed for space in here with such an outsized ego!' She slammed the door behind her.

Down in her darkroom she promptly ruined some film; it was experimental stuff, not a commission, but a crying shame all the same. Afterwards she picked up some film from Coe's, who employed her on a commission basis to do their overflow developing work, kept an appointment to photograph some clothes for a friend who ran a boutique, and headed for the city and the Holdsworth building. She discovered she had an urgent need to see Chris.

Chris Holdsworth occupied a splendid office on the twenty-fifth floor of a splendid silver building owned by Holdsworth Holdings. In the time he would occupy the even more splendid suite on the thirty-fifth floor, where his father ruled the Holdsworths' old and new money empire from the chief executive's suite. Given his father's age and his own ambitious drive, which now took him upwards at the rate of one floor a year, Chris figured he should reach the thirty-fifth and the chief executive's suite in ten years, when he would be thirty-five.

'Darling!' He ushered her into his office, where he kissed her lightly. 'This is an unexpected pleasure.'

The words were all too close an echo of the man Stevens'.

While Chris gave some instructions via his intercom, Stacey paced to the window and looked out, dissatisfied with the stupendous city—leaded spires and steel towers, cupolas, concrete rooftops and the stretching green of Hyde Park. The bronze tower of Centrepoint shot up, its turret out of sight here on the twenty-fifth floor. Chris wouldn't get a view of the turret until he was thirty-five.

'What have you been doing today, darling? Is your dress finished yet?' The question irritated her. He sounded like her father.

'I ruined some film this morning,' she told him, gazing out of the window. 'The session I did up in the mountains.'

'Never mind.' Chris came to console her. 'You can always take more pictures.'

'These were in a sun shower—the light was something else. I was hoping for some great effects.'

'There'll be other sun showers,' he said, cuddling her from behind. Stacey hid her impatience. For all that they'd been going out together these past five months, Chris still failed to understand what she did. He couldn't see that light like that was a once-only—to be in that place at that moment with those conditions. Other sun showers would never repeat the experience. She hated herself when she fouled up film. It was losing moments in time. And the reason for it was so stupid! Her tension communicated itself to Chris, who kissed her on the neck and asked if she was worrying over the party arrangements.

'It's this security man Dad's hired,' she burst out. 'He's so——' so unsettling, so interesting, so baffling, so disturbing '—so hard to take.'

'He's got a job to do. Give the poor guy a chance, darling.'

Poor guy! 'I forgot to put my alarm on last night, and he came into my bedroom while I was asleep.' She looked around at Chris, curious for his reaction.

'Sounds like an efficient fellow. Don't let it worry you. Brian wouldn't hire anyone untrustworthy. He told me this man was very experienced and not too crude.'

'Crude?' she queried.

'You know—some of these security types can be a bit seedy. Brian wouldn't want some clumsy, ignorant oaf living at the house.'

'Oh, he knows which fork to use, if that's what you mean,' said Stacey, vaguely irritated.

'Good.' Chris turned her around and kissed her. She put her arms around his neck, closed her eyes and kissed him back, thinking how very nice he smelled—of freshly laundered Swiss cotton and aftershave and, very faintly, the shampoo he'd used that morning. How civilised he was! Nothing sweaty or raw about Chris, nothing elemental and musky and outrageously, sexily male. As he kissed her, she had a mental image of Hal Stevens in boxing gloves, his shoulder and arm muscles sheened and rippling. Sharply she drew back from Chris, disguising her disquiet with false brightness. 'Hey, that aftershave is really something!'

That about summed it up, she thought on the way home. She'd never really scented the real man under Chris's aftershaves and colognes and deodorants in all the time she'd known him. Unlike Hal Stevens . . .

CHAPTER THREE

CLARE JAMIESON returned triumphant from Melbourne during the afternoon. Her second favourite designer had come up with a stunning dress. While Alex staggered upstairs under the burden of her parcels, she met Hal Stevens for the first time.

After he'd gone outside, she said to Stacey, 'I must admit to some qualms when your father said he was bringing someone in until the party. I was thinking of that dreadful man we had around while the alarm system was being changed over, remember?'

Stacey remembered. Les Howison had been dour and spoke entirely without punctuation. He'd said 'done' instead of 'did', and 'I seen' instead of 'I saw'. With polite encouragement over a Saturday luncheon, he'd offered an anecdote from his dour, dull years in security. Stacey deepened her voice and imitated Les. ' "So when I said 'I seen you do it my lad' the game was up and he broke down and confessed I like that salmon mousse——" ' Les had pronounced mousse 'mouse', and it took some few minutes to establish that he had tacked on an observation about the lunch and that the salmon rodent was not part of his shoplifter's confessional. 'I thought Les was rather fun.' Stacey grinned. 'Salmon mice and all!'

'Mmm,' her mother said as she used a letter opener on her accumulated mail. 'Mr Stevens doesn't seem too bad at all. Very dependable-looking.' She paused, read a few lines of an opened letter. 'Attractive in a way, don't you think?'

She was studiously casual, but looked hard at Stacey, who almost laughed. Her father, in blinkered masculine fashion, might remain unaware of Stevens' tough sex appeal, but her mother had recognised it immediately and was checking to ensure that her chick was not a victim to it. Stacey hesitated. *Was* she a victim to it? If she wanted to be rid of the man, all she had to do was to seem unduly interested in him, and her mother would have him out within the hour and replaced by some nice grey middle-aged man with a nice grey middle-aged manner. And wouldn't that be a whole lot more comfortable than having Hal Stevens around with his disturbing habit of turning up everywhere, wearing that expression she disliked, always making her wish for changes just because he was watching. He'd even turned Grace temporarily against her. Just how he had done it Stacey wasn't sure, but he had obviously been challenged as a 'toucher' by that lady and cleared his reputation with her. Hal had been served a superb lunch of prawns and crisp salad with Camembert and crusty bread. Stacey theoretically had the same, but her prawns and salad were indefinably dejected, her Camembert pallid, and instead of crusty bread she'd received one of the morning's batch of dinner rolls that defied all attempts to break it open. For the first time in memory Stacey had had to beg Grace's forgiveness. The housekeeper had been unusually stern, and made it clear that there was absolutely no question of Hal moving to another room, but she'd then given her a delicately crusty, delicious Danish pastry with her coffee. Forgiveness had never tasted so sweet!

Of course, it would be more comfortable without Hal Stevens around. But duller, too. She didn't want him to go—there, explain that! Her mother still watched her.

Stacey pretended to consider Hal's sex appeal. Too much interest and he would be gone in an hour, too little and he'd be gone in half that time. Her mother just would not believe that a normal, healthy woman of twenty-one would not at least notice a man like Hal.

'He's built,' she admitted, using a term she knew would make her mother wince. 'I should invite a few of the girls around while he's here—they'd appreciate his muscles. Our own tame sex-symbol,' she giggled. 'I might tell them he's my birthday present!' As she said this, Stacey suddenly wished she hadn't. It was a feeling so associated with Hal's presence that she looked at the french doors opening on to the terrace, expecting to see him. She didn't.

'Don't be crude! You talk such nonsense sometimes, Stacey,' her mother reproved, but apparently Stacey's flippancy had eased her mind, for she caught a glimpse of herself in a mirror and allowed herself to be distracted. Delicately she patted beneath her firm, youthful chin as if a dewlap trembled there. 'I look such a hag! Denise will have to give me a double appointment every day until the party, otherwise I'll be forced to wear a choker.'

Stacey laughed. Her mother was lovely, ten years younger in appearance than she ought to be, yet always fretting that her youth and looks might vanish overnight.

'Take it from me, Mother, you're not ready to join the dowager set just yet.'

Clare swept from the room with an air of satisfaction. Stacey went to the french doors and looked out on the colonnaded terrace that ran off in both directions. There was nobody there, but she felt there should have been.

*   *   *

She woke early in the morning. It was six-thirty and dawn. Another twenty minutes perhaps to sunrise. Stacey took a look from the window and decided it would be a crime to waste that light. Instead of going along to the sitting-room to compose a mnemonic for the Millers' carriage clock, she ran downstairs barefooted. Hal's door was closed; the watchdog was probably fast asleep. In the cellar she picked up a camera and lens bag, and let herself out into the back garden via the flower-room. It was a dewy winter morning. The sun found tiny rainbows in drying droplets on the lawn. Close-clipped hedges zigzagged along an arbour path to hug the tennis court. Jamieson House, though it had lost much of its original grounds at the turn of the century, still kept its distance from neighbours, and, though the unimpeded Harbour views had gone with the acreage, there were still glimpses of water to be had through the oak and magnolia branches. The house's massive back terrace, which overhung the free-form swimming pool, was high enough to make a spectacular vantage point for the start of the Sydney-Hobart yacht race every Boxing Day, when hundreds of sails swept through the Heads to the open sea.

Stacey checked the light, used the outstretched arm of a nude female sculpture to steady the Nikon, and focused the 200mm lens on the diamond-faceted conservatory. In the early light some of its panes were molten bronze, some silver. Adding a filter, she crouched down for a new angle and did a bracket of shots, altering the exposure each time, then walked on, looking for some new discovery in the familiarity of her own back garden. Her robe dragged along the stone pool-edges. She bent and dipped her fingers in the water, confirming that it was as icy as it looked. Her father was surprisingly parsimonious about some things. He refused to heat the pool in June and July, claiming it an unwarranted expense for one or two winter swims.

As she emerged on to the stretch of lawn beyond the tennis court, a movement caught her eye. Hal Stevens was not asleep, after all. He was here. It was an eye-catching tableau—him in black track-suit pants with red side stripes and the sleeveless black sweat-shirt, caught in hazed morning light, bordered by Mr Jaswinsky's hedges. Against the lime green of the foliage and the golden-dewed grass he stood out in bold reflief, his hair falling over his forehead and curling damply at his temples. Stacey's heartbeat picked up. This certainly was a new discovery at the bottom of the garden! She ducked back behind cover, adjusting her lens, hoping he hadn't noticed her. After a moment she peeped out, but he was still intent on his workout. Smiling, she raised the camera. She would get her pictures of him, after all. A sitting would have been nice but, now that she thought about it, candids could be even better.

She became absorbed, zoomed in and previewed the close-up of Hal, his face a study in concentration, eyes rock-steady and fixed on some inner vision. A couple of shots she squeezed off, tensing at each faint click and electronic wind-on. But he didn't hear it and he didn't see her. Stacey laughed silently. Hawk-eye Hal was so busy practising his martial arts that he didn't even know she had him in her sights! Removing the 200mm lens, she switched to wide-angle and studied this new perspective, which placed the controlled energy of the man against the backdrop of ordered tranquillity.

There was a strong relationship between him and his surroundings. He closed his eyes, breathed deeply in a meditative way, then performed a series of kicks—

whirling, lethal kicks in swift succession. Stacey grinned. No sign of a limp. She got some of it at a fast speed to freeze the action, then changed down to capture the movement at the expense of clarity. My, my, he *did* look dangerous! Her shoulders shook. And she could be a burglar sneaking up on the house and he wouldn't even know. She could nip in through the open kitchen door and make off with a bagful of the smaller stuff while he was down here practising his drop kicks. Wouldn't that be classic? It would almost be worth losing the presents to see the look on his face. Stacey lowered the camera and her grin broadened.

'Oh, Stacey, you wouldn't!' But she thought of herself unwittingly stripping while he watched, and her smile firmed maliciously. 'Oh, Stacey, you *would!*'

Carefully she set the camera down beneath a budding camellia, and loosened the belt of her robe a little to look awry. Then, schooling her face into shock and anxiety, she ran across the grass to him.

'Mr Stevens——' she called breathlessly, as if she'd raced downstairs to find him. No, no—in the shock of a break-in she would dispense with formality, she was sure. 'Hal—*Hal!*'

He whirled around, knees bent and hands spread, Action Man at the ready. He took in her bare feet, the dishevelled gown and her flying hair.

'What is it?' he snapped out.

'I called you—where *were* you? There's a man——' she panted artistically, 'in the house—he——' She had no time to finish. Hal came for her and almost swept her off her feet, running with her to the tennis shelter, an arm around her waist. Her breath was coming in genuine gasps when he wheeled her inside and pushed her behind him. With narrowed eyes, he raked the upstairs windows and terrace.

'How the hell——?' he muttered. 'There's no way anyone could have . . . dammit! I shouldn't have come outside. Where was he?'

Stacey's lips quivered. He felt guilty for deserting his post. Good. 'I didn't know what to do and you weren't in your room or anywhere around——' she said, laying it on thick. 'I just caught a glimpse of him in the west gallery. What are you going to do? Are you going after him?' she gasped, clutching at his arm as if she was terrified. His skin was hot and damp, and he smelled earthy.

'The west gallery? I would have thought . . .' His body was tense, crouched.

'Thank goodness I found you,' she gabbled. If only she could keep a straight face! 'I thought Dad was being paranoid about a burglary, but it just shows——'

'Burglary!' Hal bit out. He took her by the shoulders. 'Look, I want you to stay here, understand? Don't move. If anyone gets past me I want you to scream like hell and hightail it to Alex, got it?'

'Hightail it to Alex,' she repeated breathlessly, gazing into his eyes. 'Got it.' She almost laughed. Hightail it, for heaven's sake! He must get his dialogue from television. She poked her head out of the shelter to see him, doubled over, running from hedge to hedge, tree to tree, as if there were snipers on the terrace. Stacey giggled, then bit her lip. As Hal froze behind the nude sculpture, her giggle turned to laughter and escaped. The sound flowed across the garden, and Hal turned his head to see her in full view, leaning against the tennis shelter, laughing helplessly. She clapped her hands in slow, mock applause. 'That was *very* good, Mr Stevens,' she called, and broke up again. After a moment he rose to his feet and walked back to her. 'You handled that with great panache,' she chortled. 'Nerves of steel, instant reflexes, faster than a speeding bullet——'

Her head jolted back as he laid those big hands on her shoulders and jerked her once. 'You stupid little bitch!' he growled.

Stacey opened her eyes wide at him. 'Relax,' she said, as he had that night in her room. 'There's no intruder. It's only me.'

'You made it up! Why, you spoiled, selfish brat——'

'Now, now—could you abuse me quietly?' she chided. Her hair fell forward as he shook her.

'You think it's all a game! Are you so bloody bored that you——' He bit off his words angrily, took a deep breath and closed his eyes.

'Now, Mr Stevens—a good security man never closes his eyes,' she mocked. He literally flung her away from him and stumped into the tennis shed. He must feel an idiot. Not quite the idiot she'd felt, but pretty silly. Something niggled at her—something not quite right, but she couldn't place it. No matter. Stacey followed him into the shed to witness his humiliation. She hadn't had so much fun in ages.

'So it was just a little joke?' he said, calmer. Disappointingly calm.

Shrugging, she sat down on the bench and crossed her legs, smiling at him. 'You can take a joke, can't you?'

Hal stripped off his damp shirt, crumpled it into a ball and flung it on the bench next to her, where his towel and jacket lay. 'Sure I can take a joke. I should have stopped to wonder why you came racing out to me instead of raising the alarm from the house. But you were very convincing. You're quite an actress.' He looked almost admiring.

'That's what I like, a good sport,' she grinned.

'Oh, is *that* what you like?' Bare-chested, he leaned

past her and took the towel. His distinctive, pleasant
scent strengthened. Stacey was sure she could pick him
out in a crowd blindfolded. Her pulse skittered about as
she watched him towel himself. There was a sheen on his
skin and a felting of damp, dark hair on his chest. He
leaned past yet again to pick up his jacket and throw
down the towel. Yet there was a gleam in his eyes that
took away the symbolism of that last. Stacey didn't like
the look of it. It might be prudent to leave while she was
points ahead. But when she got up to go a heavy hand
descended on her shoulder.

'Don't go,' he said pleasantly, and zipped his jacket
to the half-way mark.

'I have to——' She stood again, and again went down
like a yo-yo. 'Hey, what *is* this?' she glared, but was
rendered speechless when Hal knelt one leg across her
thighs to keep her immobile. From his pocket he
produced a comb and flicked it through his hair, and
Stacey recovered sufficiently to shove at his leg. But his
thigh was as unyielding as a tree-trunk. He pocketed the
comb. 'Now,' he said, releasing her.

Stacey shot up, but the moment she was standing he
stooped, seized her under the knees and around the
waist, and she was airborne and out in the sunlight.
'What are you doing?' she yelled, trying to kick, push at
his shoulders and hold together the edges of her robe
simultaneously. 'Let me go!'

'I intend to,' he promised, tipping his head aside to
avoid her flailing arm. That was when she noticed where
he was walking—right along the meandering edge of the
pool. All the way along it, to the deep end. Stacey
reversed her strategy and clutched at him instead of
pushing. His body generated so much warmth. The pool
was so cold. 'No! No, you wouldn't,' she croaked. 'You
wouldn't! The water's freezing!'

'Come on, be a sport, Stacey.'

'You rotten pig, you can't do this—eek!' The icy aqua water came into view beneath her and she climbed up him, clinging on like a koala.

'That won't do you any good. I can shake you off, no trouble. Now, take a deep breath—I suppose you *can* swim? I wouldn't like to have to come in to rescue you. But of course you can swim,' he answered himself.

'You're bluffing!'

'And a-one——' He swung her out over the water.

'Aahh—it was just a joke, you big bully, don't you *dare*——' Her hand scrabbled, caught at his jacket zipper, pulling it down.

Tch, tch, now is no time to be unwrapping your birthday present, Miss Stacey,' he chided.

'You *heard* that?' she gasped. Her feeling had been right, then.

'Yes, I heard. But I forgive you for that. I'm throwing you in for this morning's bitchery . . . and a-*two*——' Another swing out.

'I didn't mean that about you being my birthday present,' she babbled, sure she'd found the key to salvation. 'I was just kidding around——'

'And a-*three!*'

'You rotten, lousy—oh, no! No! Hal, don't let me go. *Please* don't let me go——' she begged. She had both arms around his neck now, and even when he set her feet on the ground again she didn't let go. Nor did he release her immediately. In the struggle her gown had come adrift, and his jacket gaped open. Her face pressed into his shoulder, and with relief came a sudden rush of awareness, as if her nervous system was shouting out the headlines. Read all about it—smooth, heated skin, springy body hair, Hal's heart thumping against her, his ribcage rising and falling, his breath

warm on her neck. His hands slid down her back to her
waist and he lifted her away, took her arms from his
neck. Brown eyes almost black, opaque, shuttered.

Stacey stared at him, opening her mouth a little to
take a deep breath. She held it. The niggling feeling of
something not quite right exploded into a dozen
different impressions. Negatives and positives. Hal
whirling to meet her, his eyes sweeping the house and
garden. Hal shielding her with his body as he bundled
her into the shelter. Hal always around, watching. Hal
in her bedroom, and her father and Chris condoning it.
Alex wanting to know where she went and how long she
would be, agitated that no one could keep up with her
driving. Grace, so quickly convinced that Hal should
occupy the room next to hers. They must have let her in
on it, then. Her mother, of course, was in the dark, too.

'You're here to protect *me,* aren't you?' she said.

Hal scanned the pub's lunchtime crowd and pulled a
chair out for Stacey. As he sat down, he casually let his
eyes drift around the tables. Light rain had begun to
fall, and groups of patrons out in the courtyard
gathered up their food and drinks to move inside. He
looked at each face.

'Nothing's happened. Nothing has even looked like
happening,' Stacey said. 'You don't really take those
notes seriously?'

She had found amusement in his vigilance this last
week. Since she had discovered he was actually guarding
her and not her birthday baubles, all pretence had been
dropped and he'd been appointed full-time bodyguard,
which meant he'd had the joy of following the brat
around to a succession of beauty parlours, hairdressers,
boutiques, antique fairs and avant-garde art galleries—
all regular haunts of hers, but he suspected she'd

stepped up her attendance at them just to bore him to tears. His eyes came around to her face.

'You don't believe anyone could possibly wish you harm?' he said drily. The threats had been sent to her father—the usual anonymous pastings of cut-out letters and words from magazines, rambling on about filthy capitalist swine who spent money on racehorses for their darling daughters while the masses struggled to pay the rent. Two letters. The one that had really put the wind up Brian actually mentioned Stacey by name. 'Happy birthday, Miss Stacey Jamieson. Gift follows.' It had a sinister sound, that 'gift follows'. It could mean anything from a whoopee cushion in the mail to a kidnap and ransom attempt. Just the sight of his daughter's name had brought Brian out in a cold sweat. Clare Jamieson had almost swooned when she was finally told about the threats. Not so her daughter. When Stacey was shown the notes, she tossed them aside, scornfully bracketing them with the hundreds of other crank letters her father had received in the past.

'Why should anyone wish me harm?' she queried now.

'To know you isn't necessarily to love you, sweetheart. You've had a lot of publicity lately. Your father bought that racehorse and you were pictured with it. The gossip columns are totting up the price tag for your party already—a lot of people out there who have nothing might resent that.'

'It's just some weirdo who has nothing better to do,' she shrugged. 'But that's OK. It's quite a novel experience to have a bodyguard.' She threw back her head and smiled saucily at him. It was a new game for her—the heiress and the bodyguard. Hal shook his head. Pampered and protected from birth, the girl just couldn't believe that anything bad would happen. It was why she'd been so offhand about the near-accident on the drive, he decided. She wasn't so much callous as certain her life was charmed. Not for a moment had she thought she'd injured him. It didn't fit the pattern of a charmed life. It was a dangerous illusion.

'Do you think you'll only ever have sunshine, Stacey—no rain?' he asked.

To his surprise she sobered and looked away, as if he'd reminded her of something. She sucked in the corner of her lower lip, something she did now and then. It was a sign he'd come to recognise—a sign that occasionally something serious went on in her head. For a while there, when she'd discovered that her father had had her followed when she went out, watched at home without her knowing, she had felt a fool. Her father, of course, fobbed her off with his usual hearty, paternal guff about not wanting to worry her sweet head and spoil her party for her, et cetera, et cetera, which really meant she had no say in the matter at all. Later she'd said to Hal, 'I suppose you think I'm stupid, not noticing that I was being protected.'

'You don't notice what's always there,' he had replied, wondering if she could really be unaware that her protection, while it might not always entail a body-guard, was a full-time thing and not just a reaction to the threats. Did she realise she was a pretty puppet decked out like her mother in the symbols of Brian Jamieson's success, while he pulled the strings? Couldn't she see that her father was pushing her towards marriage with Holdsworth and his old money connections to achieve his nouveau-riche ambitions? Probably not. If a girl in a poor family was manipulated so shamelessly, she would notice, but the trappings of wealth gave Stacey the illusion of freedom and choice. She'd chewed a bit at her lip that time too, as if what he'd said rang a bell somewhere in that lovely head of hers.

This time she chewed a bit longer, then said absently, 'I can't remember any rain when I was little. I remember all those holidays at the beach, but I can't remember any rain.'

'Your father probably arranged for fine weather,' he said, tongue in cheek. Stacey's green eyes switched to him. They looked disturbed, thoughtful—a long way from the teasing, laughing, malicious, imperious expressions he'd come to expect. They also looked beautiful—deep green with a touch of blue, flecked with gold. She was a pain, but she was beautiful. And sometimes fun. Hal looked away, grateful when the waiter came with their drinks. From habit, he scanned the crowd again.

'What do you look for?' she asked, leaning her chin on her hand.

'A face that's cropped up before—someone tense. The signs are there when you know what to look for. Someone who's showing a lot of interest in you.' He gave a wry smile. 'There are plenty of those, but so far all just normal, red-blooded males ogling a gorgeous girl.'

'I'm surprised to hear *you* describe me like that!'

He grinned. She was fishing. 'I'm merely saying that *they* think you're gorgeous. They wouldn't if they had to look after you.'

'I haven't been nice to you, have I?' she reflected. 'Would you like me to be nice to you?'

'I'm not sure I could take the shock,' said Hal, regarding her suddenly intense gaze with wariness. She telegraphed every move. That should make it simple for him to keep out of her way.

'How old are you, Hal?' she asked.

'Twenty-nine.'

'Do you have any brothers and sisters?'

Gravely, he told her—two brothers and a sister.

'Are you like your father to look at?'

'Nope. My father's generally considered to be a handsome devil.'

'You're not handsome, but you're very—striking,' she conceded. She studied him with unnerving frankness. 'I wish you'd let me photograph you.'

'I'd make a lousy model. If you intend taking any photographs over the next few days, I'd recommend interiors rather than exteriors, from a safety point of view.' But whose safety are we talking about? he thought derisively. The steak dinners came. Thank God for eating and drinking, they provided excellent diversions.

'Don't change the subject,' she protested, shaking out her paper napkin. 'We were talking about you.'

'I'm your bodyguard until your father decides otherwise, Stacey,' he said pleasantly. 'Let's not complicate things.'

'What does that mean?'

'If you're bored with Holdsworth, perhaps you'd better dump him and try someone more red-blooded. But not me.'

She flushed. 'You? You think I'm interested in you because I ask you a few questions?' Her eyes flashed, her hair rippled as she shook it back angrily. He tore his eyes away from it, shrugged.

'Just an impression.'

'But *you,* of course, are not interested in *me.*' She was haughty now, on her dignity. And still fishing.

'You're wrong. I'm extremely interested in you and your safety.'

'But not as a woman?'

Talk about persistence! Most women would have taken the hint and started talking about the weather by now. It was one of her most irritating features, yet oddly her frank, almost childish curiosity was part of her appeal. In spite of her background, there was a certain lack of artifice in her manner.

'As a woman?' he laughed. 'Ask me that when you *are* one. If you ever are.'

Stacey tore into her lunch, sawing at her steak so vigorously that the three-legged table rocked. 'You are the most insulting man——!'

'You only think so because I tell you the truth. You're not used to it.'

She wasn't listening. '—not true, anyway.' She slashed an Idaho potato in half. Little bits of foil fluttered on to the table. 'Chris is no wimp . . . but you know that. You watched closely enough when we said goodnight last night.'

'It wasn't exactly *Gone with the Wind*,' mocked Hal. She and Holdsworth had gone to a party last night, and Holdsworth hadn't been happy at all to have the body-guard along. In fact, the man's prickly reaction to him made Hal wonder what Stacey had said about him. Something inventive, he supposed—something on a par with the 'toucher' story she'd told by implication to Grace Warman. The goodnight kiss had turned into a definite 'hands off' demonstration by one man to another. Holdsworth could have been branding a cow, so obvious had it been. 'And his blood is more on the blue side. That's why your father is so keen to have him in the family.'

'Don't be ridiculous!' she scoffed.

'If you don't marry Holdsworth, you'll marry someone just like him, which would be a pity.'

'Oh? And why is that?' She waved a fork full of

salad, and a few shreds of alfalfa fell to the table.

'You could be quite a woman. But you'll exchange one golden cage for another. Holdsworth or another clone will take over from your daddy and keep you safe from the nasties and things that go bump in the night, and you'll never find out that you can't have the things that matter without risks.'

'The suspense is killing me! What *are* these things that matter—in your opinion?' Stacey opened her eyes wide at him.

'Independence, usefulness. Freedom,' he said, feeling a rush of sympathy for her. Her father's ambition and fears had shaped her life so far, and a husband's ambition and fears would shape it in the future. Poor little rich girl!

CHAPTER FOUR

STACEY'S plate was a battlefield. Remnants of steak went furiously under the knife, and she kept pushing portions in her mouth, chewing fast and swallowing in between talking. Well-bred girls did not talk with their mouths full. Hal found the adherence to the rule, even at this pinnacle of anger, quite unexpectedly endearing.

'And why should marriage be a cage?' Stacey demanded. 'I would expect to combine marriage with a career if I wanted.'

'What career is that?' he asked mildly.

'Photography.' She glared and shoved food into her mouth to grind it up ready for her next riposte.

'You think Holdsworth would like a wife trotting around taking pictures?' He watched with amusement as she desperately tried to finish chewing to answer. Manners decreed that every scrap must be disposed of first. He thought about the photographs she had pinned up outside her darkroom. They seemed quite good to him. Some of her subject matter was surprising. 'For instance, what about that study of the derelict with the *boutonnière?* Not the sort of thing a nice society matron chooses to photograph. How did you get that, by the way?'

Clearly, she was torn between a wish to tell him to mind his own business or talk about her camera work. The amateur photographer won. Grudgingly she explained that she'd been photographing the flower-sellers in Martin Place early one morning, and had seen old Barney pick up a short-stemmed carnation from the ground and slip it into the buttonhole of his frayed, filthy jacket. 'But the pictures I got then weren't what I wanted, so I talked to the flower-sellers and they said he came by every morning. If he didn't find a broken flower to wear one of the sellers gave him one. So I went back every morning and waited for just the right shot . . .'

And she'd got it, Hal thought. The arches and columns of the General Post Office, soft grey in the morning light, tight bunches of gold and white and rust chrysanthemums, posies of violets and glowing spears of carmine gladioli. And the derelict Barney caught in a moment of grace, tucking the flower into his shabby lapel—a sort of captured ritual of dignity in an undignified life. Yes, it was just the right shot, and it gave her satisfaction. Temporarily she forgot to glare. Her knife and fork were still, her dinner spared for the moment. There was a dreamy look in her eyes—beautiful eyes. Damn the girl, why did she have to have unexpected depths? Why couldn't she have looked like her old man? Heiresses had enough going for them without eyes like those and hair like that and a mouth . . . 'How many times did you go back to get the picture you wanted?' he asked.

'Oh, about nine or ten, I think——'

'Nine or ten. You think Holdsworth is going to let his lovely wife lurk about town in the early hours for a fortnight to take snaps of tramps?'

'Will you stop assuming I'm marrying Holdswor— Chris! It isn't a question of anyone *letting* me do anything.' The cutlery was back in action again, rattling like a harvester on her plate. 'I'll do what I want.'

'Then you'll have to make some changes.' Hal regretted saying that. In fact, he wished he could erase most of this exchange. He had vowed to remain outside all this, and here he was trying to hold up a mirror for her to see how she looked in her cocoon. Damned fool! The girl probably wanted to be in it, wanted to stay in it. Somehow he'd let himself get involved. You're here to guard the body, that's all, he reminded himself. How about re-phrasing that? 'Body' conjured up images of Stacey twirling naked in her moonlit room. The goods; he was here to guard the goods. That was better. He glanced around the pub again, smiled at Stacey, who glowered back at him. Her eyes flicked up at something behind him and he tensed. When someone grabbed him from behind, the adrenalin pounded into his system. He reached beneath his jacket, had the gun almost out in the open when a familiar voice said huskily, 'Hal!'

He shoved the weapon back, but not before Stacey had glimpsed it. Inwardly he cursed. He might not want her to totally disregard the threats, but neither did he want her frightened and hysterical. Her eyes remained wide and fixed on the spot where she had glimpsed the gun. When she looked up at Hal, it was with the usual reaction. Fear of the weapon itself—and of a man who would carry it. Damn! He'd assumed she would expect a bodyguard to be armed, but he should have told her. Damn!

'It's so good to see you, Hal!' The arms about his neck were warm and generous. He felt a rush of affection.

'Linda,' he croaked, disengaging her arms, 'stop strangling me and give me a kiss.'

Stacey stared at Hal as he stood. She hardly saw the girl who laughingly kissed him on the mouth. That Hal might carry a weapon had never crossed her mind. And the way he'd reached for it . . . it jolted her that he might have been prepared to brandish it, even use it. It repelled her. It cut through her complacency. The most she'd felt about the notes was a queasiness that some crank would cut the letters of her name from a magazine. Now, with the snub barrel of that gun etched in her mind, knowing that Hal thought it a necessary precaution, the threats seemed much more serious. She glanced all around as Hal had done, her eyes flicking nervously from one face to another. They all seemed so ordinary, so normal, yet maybe one of these people snipped bits out of magazines and planned the demise of innocent girls.

It was all so fantastic. Someone might try to hurt her, even try to kill her; yet, even with the notes and her father's anxiety, it had never really crossed her mind. She looked out at the rain pouring down on empty tables and umbrellas. There were a lot of things that had never crossed her mind until lately. She must be what the experts called a late developer. Too fast, she tossed back some wine, and choked. Hal looked around as she coughed and spluttered, and gave her what she supposed was meant to be a reassuring smile. Balefully she regarded him through watering eyes, her fear converted to resentment as the girl twined around him came into focus. So much for *his* protection! It was probably safe enough in a busy place like this, but if someone did try anything they had a good chance with her bodyguard's hands full. Sourly, she ran her eyes over the girl. Very full. More a woman than a girl was Linda. Not exactly pretty, and her figure was definitely overripe. Still, she apparently considered herself youthful enough to wear her hair long to her waist, and dress like a teenager in cotton trousers, drawstring cheesecloth blouse and a cerise and turquoise jumper which was tied by the sleeves around her neck.

'You look terrific, you sexy devil!' Linda tightened

her arms about Hal in a little hug. 'What are you doing these days? Still teaching karate with darling Mick? Oh——' she plucked at the hand-knitted blue sweater he wore under his jacket '—you're wearing the jumper I knitted for you, sentimental fool.' She dealt him an affectionate buff on one shoulder. 'Did you ever buy that land for your farm? You *did?*' Another hug. 'Congratulations!'

She was holding him tight enough to feel the gun, surely, Stacey thought. But, if so, it didn't put her off. Hal's arms were loosely around her and he laughed down at Linda with such warmth, such genuine liking, that Stacey felt almost jealous. She'd never seen him look like this. When he finally turned to her, she scowled at him.

'Linda, this is Stacey,' he said, directing a swift look around the pub.

'Hi.' Linda extended a hand and gave Stacey a comprehensive look. 'Are you two——?' She crossed two fingers cosily. Hal just smiled and shook his head.

'We have a very simple relationship,' Stacey told her. 'He's only interested in my body.'

Linda appeared to find that surprising. Stacey couldn't decide if it was an insult to her or a compliment to Hal. He pulled out a chair and Linda sat down. Wonderful, Stacey thought.

'Hal, come on, tell me what's happening down on the farm. Have you started building Hal's Health Hideaway yet?'

He laughed. 'I've decided to keep the old homestead name—Cedar Hill—so as not to discourage the general tourist trade.'

Linda rolled her eyes. 'They'll suspect something, you know, when they sit down to chick peas and bean-sprouts for breakfast.'

Stacey got lost in this conversation, but gradually pried loose the interesting fact that Hal owned forty acres of land with a farmhouse on it, that he planned to develop into a health farm, with special emphasis on rest, training and rehabilitation for sportsmen and women. The catering was to be flexible enough to include ordinary holidaymakers who wanted a tranquil location and hearty country-style meals.

It was in northern New South Wales, and Linda appeared to know quite a lot about it. Stacey got the impression that Cedar Hill was a long-standing ambition of Hal's. She studied him covertly. A man full of surprises—police force, security work at Talisman, martial arts instructor, bodyguard and entrepreneur. As Linda plied him with questions about his health farm, he grew gradually more and more enthusiastic. He cleared a space on the table in front of him and arranged his cutlery on it to demonstrate the position of the creek and the present farmhouse.

'I'll use the old place for accommodation temporarily, but it will be demolished once the resort is built. Of course, I've yet to raise the money, but it's a good proposition and it won't be too difficult to get when I'm ready——'

His hands shaped and closed and stretched to create the vision of Cedar Hill. His dream was already built in his mind. He reached over and took Stacey's plate, which became the main resort and gymnasium. The pepper and salt shakers represented ten guest cabins. Tennis courts, pool, sauna, spas were located in front of Linda, who gazed down rapturously, as if she could really see them as Hal obviously could. Their oneness irritated Stacey, who felt sour at being left out.

At last he looked up. Just for a moment he looked at Stacey, his brown eyes open wide with fervour over his plans. Then his eyes cleared and the boyishness disappeared. There followed another ten minutes from which Stacey was excluded, while they chatted about Linda's recent appointment as lecturer in Ancient History at the University of New South Wales, and her trip last year to Greece and her decision to take bouzouki lessons as a direct result of that. Stacey had to admit she sounded like a fun girl. Woman.

At length, Linda grabbed Hal's hand and twisted around to look at his watch. 'Have to go. Lovely seeing you.' She grinned, plucking at the blue sweater again. 'It's wearing almost as well as you, you hunk. 'Bye, Stacey,' she said, pausing to look her over speculatively. Stacey had the feeling that she was being assessed as a worthy partner for Hal, and coming out of it on the minus side. It was confirmed when Linda leaned forward impulsively and said, 'He's one of a kind, even if he is a bit stubborn sometimes.' Treat him right, her eyes seemed to be saying to Stacey. Linda's feelings for him clearly ran deep. After she'd gone, a smile lingered about Hal's mouth and he wore a reminiscent look that nettled Stacey.

'She's a lousy knitter,' she said. He focused on her as if he'd forgotten she was there. 'She made it too tight.' She indicated the weave that was stretched across his chest.

'But she made it. I suppose she could have bought one in a shop which would have been less trouble,' he said sarcastically, 'or she could have given me the money to buy one, which would have been even less bother.'

It was a reminder of her casual offer to replace his other jumper, ruined on the drive on his first day. 'You surely didn't expect me to *knit* you a replacement?' she demanded.

'I surely didn't,' he drawled, as if anything so useful

was bound to be beyond her. And, gallingly, it was. Her expensive education hadn't included knitting. He paused, did his slow scan again and brought his gaze back to her. 'I'm sorry if you were frightened by the gun. I thought you'd take it for granted that I would be armed. When Linda grabbed me like that I acted on reflex. It's a while since I've done a job like this, and I'm a little edgy, I suppose. That's nothing for you to worry about. A little edginess is good in this business.'

The reassuring tone riled her. 'Would you have used it?' She swallowed a bit at the idea. He'd learned about firearms in the police force, she supposed.

'Only as a last resort,' he said. 'If you were in mortal danger.'

'You'd wait until I was in mortal danger first?' she said in mock protest, but her voice trembled a bit now that she was reminded of the gun and the danger. She supposed those other security people her father had employed at the house in the past had carried guns, but she'd never seen one. Not once. She looked outside at the wet, empty tables. She couldn't remember any rain. She'd never seen any guns. 'What about if I was in extreme danger? Say the villain has me by the throat, one foot on a cliff and the other scrabbling around for a foothold?'

She saw his surprise and the answering flick of humour in his eyes. 'No worries. I have a knife for extreme danger.'

'What about serious danger?'

His eyebrows went up. 'Two feet on the cliff? Serious danger's a cosh,' he said. 'Anything less than serious I use my bare hands.' He mimed a wringing motion, and Stacey laughed, grateful that he'd seen her need to deal with the situation by making fun of it.

'Do you really have a knife?'

Gravely Hal pulled out a penknife and snapped open the tiny blade. 'It's great for sharpening pencils,' he protested when she scoffed at it.

'If someone comes at me with an HB I've got no worries, then,' she smiled.

Hal sent a staying glance her way when she made to pay for the lunch. Shrugging, she watched him thumb out some notes. 'You and Linda must have been very good friends,' she observed.

'Very good friends,' he agreed. 'We lived together for a time. It didn't work out, but I wish it had.'

Lovers. Live-in lovers. Stacey imagined it quickly, as if she was doing a photo session on it. Quick little flashes of Hal and Linda cooking together, laughing in bed, his head close to hers, her long brown hair swathed across his chest as he shared his dreams with her . . . such clarity in those pictures. Lord, she was jealous! It was ridiculous.

'If you've finished, I have an appointment to keep,' she said abruptly. 'It's not part of your job to sit around rambling about your farm and catching up with old girlfriends.'

Hal's mouth tightened. 'Thank you, brat. I need to be reminded every now and then what a spoiled little bitch you really are. It makes it so much easier.' Whatever that meant. He crumpled his paper napkin and tossed it down. The flimsy table jolted as he stood, and her plate nearly fell off.

'Careful,' she drawled. 'You nearly wiped out your gymnasium!'

She wished she hadn't spoiled the very nice mood they had had going between them. Wish, wish, she thought. Always when Hal was around she had cause for regret. She should apologise. Stacey sneaked a look at Hal's granite face. Words of apology did not come easy to

her, and he didn't look receptive. She said nothing.
They were outside in the rain when she noticed he was
limping again.

Her appointment was at a boutique. Since her early
teens she'd been a model for charity fashion parades,
and this shop often supplied clothes to be modelled. The
next event was a 'fashion extravaganza' aboard
someone's yacht. Stacey thought it a bit risky herself.
High heels and high seas could be a disastrous combination, even with the promised carpeted catwalk. Two
other volunteer models were already there, and
Monique, the owner, glamorous in black, her arms full
of fashion, greeted Stacey with a skimming little kiss on
the cheek. Hal she regarded speculatively.

'Stacey darling, all your size tens are on the rack in
the dressing-room.' The batwing doors leading to the
cubicles flipped and flapped behind her.

'I'll be an hour or so, I expect,' Stacey said to Hal,
and waved a hand around at the racks of dresses, suits,
ballgowns and lingerie. 'You won't be too bored, will
you?'

He caught her arm as she made to follow Monique. 'I
take it there's a back entrance via the dressing-room?'

'Yes—it leads to the parking space in a lane——'

He nodded and she moved on, putting out a hand to
the batwing doors. Hal was right at her heels. 'You
can't come in,' she said over her shoulder. 'Ladies
only.'

'You did say this was an appointment made—how
long ago?'

She shrugged. 'Oh, weeks.'

'Which means quite a few people would know or
could find out that you'll be here today at this time.'

'Don't be silly! Nobody I know would have written
those notes . . .' Stacey's voice trailed off at his unyield-

ing look. Nervously, she glanced beyond him. The boutique, usually only frightening for its avant-garde designer clothes, suddenly took on sinister overtones. 'You can wait by the back door, then,' she said abruptly, to hide the irrational flash of fear.

'And neglect the shop entrance?' he queried. 'I'll come in where I can see you or any visitors.'

'But you *can't* come in! How will I explain that?'

Hal's smile was an echo of her malicious one. 'You're such an inventive little soul,' he said. 'You'll think of something.'

Monique gave an amused little scream. 'He can't come in here, darling!' Two women popped their heads over the cubicle doors. One gave a little gasp of surprise; the other merely raised her brows and flipped a strapless bra over the door. Eyes on Hal, she said, 'I need a bigger size, Monique.'

'But darling—I mean, he's perfectly delicious, of course,' said Monique with an appreciative glance at Hal, 'but why bring him in here?'

Hal took the compliment without a blink, crossed his arms and leaned on the wall. He was enjoying himself, Stacey thought darkly, trying to come up with a reason to drag a man into the fitting-room with her. She couldn't say he was a bodyguard; it would be in the papers the next day. She was in the hot seat and his ego, was being stroked by Monique and that man-eater Pauline, who was sending him eye-signals that needed no decoding. Even Jennie had recovered from her surprise and was smiling at him as she zipped herself into something behind the cubicle door. Hal raised a brow and waited raptly for her reply. She lowered her lids. But she was an inventive little soul.

'Oh, Monique darling, he *has* to stay,' she said in a spoiled young thing voice. 'He's my hairdresser.' She gave Hal a big smile, and he blinked rapidly a few times. 'He wants to see exactly what I'm to wear so he can do something really fabulous with my hair on the night. It'll do terrific things for your clothes, I promise you——'

Monique and the others studied Hal's dynamic appearance sceptically. With his jeans and the hand-knitted sweater and his bulky battle jacket clinging to his big shoulders and biceps, he looked as if he'd just spent six months hacking his way through darkest Africa rather than snipping at hair!

'It's all right, Monique—honestly. He's practically one of us.' Stacey tacked on a meaningful little smile and took her hangers from the rack. Inside her cubicle she met Hal's eyes challengingly over the door. He straightened from the wall and for a moment she thought he was going to deny her implication and wait outside. Instead, he set one hand on his hip and wandered over to the clothes rack to delicately finger some red shot taffeta.

Monique sighed. 'Oh, all right, he can stay.'

Pauline sighed too and hauled in her bra. And Hal stayed, fiendishly eyeing Stacey over the top of the door as she changed. Her face reddened as she stripped off to the waist for a ghastly mustard strapless number. How much could he see from the vantage point of his height? She was stuck with the pretence, of course, and each time she emerged for Monique to check the fit of an outfit, Hal managed a very creditable imitation of Ramón, whom he'd seen in action on her hair twice now.

'Sideswept, I think, Stacey sweet,' he said once, plunging his fingers into her hair to draw it to one side. He pulled on it a bit to punish her, and her eyes watered as they met his in the mirrored wall. Her hair spilled from Hal's big hands, her eyes locked with his and their game-playing was momentarily suspended. He was close behind her; she could feel the brush of his wool jacket against her bare back and he seemed to be drawing her backwards, closer into the curve of his shoulders. Then, abruptly, his pressure on her scalp eased. He released her hair and smoothed it—not the way Ramón did it, lacing his fingers professionally through it, but softly, intently, his fingertips straying on to her face and neck. Her nerves leapt up at each tiny touch, shouting the news: this is wonderful. His hands are so beautiful to watch, like works of art. Without looking up again at her reflection in the mirror, Hal set his hands heavily on her shoulders and turned her towards the changing cubicle.

He made no further effort to behave like a hairdresser, and when they were outside again he was courteously distant. And he still limped. Stacey pulled up the hood of her trenchcoat against the rain which had strengthened, but Hal merely turned up his collar, stuck his hands in his pockets and hunched down as they went to the car. By the time they were inside, his hair was soaked and dripping over his face and neck.

'Aren't *you* the one who should have the trenchcoat?' laughed Stacey, folding down her hood.

'You're thinking of private eyes,' he grunted, mopping at his face with a handkerchief. 'Trenchcoats went out with Sam Spade and Mike Hammer.'

'Hang on——' said Stacey, and slewed around in her seat to delve into her camera bag on the floor behind her seat. With a hand towel clutched in one hand, she came up with a jolt and some assistance from Hal. There was no space to spare in the sports car. Hal's face was close to hers as she held the towel up between them. He didn't take it at once, but just looked at her with a sort of quiet ferociousness that made her nervous—breathless, as if she'd been running hard. The car windows were awash with silver-grey and the wet-on-wet green of a street tree and the blue of a passing umbrella. The rain surrounded them, muted the traffic noise, muffled the sound of hurrying feet, turned the outside into a water-colour fantasy. Stacey stared at Hal, his hair dark and slick with water, his eyes deepest brown, almost black, his craggy cheekbones and the grainy, hollowed-out planes beneath glistening with moisture. She tracked a runnel of water down to his mouth—such an interesting mouth, tilting down one side, denting in the other . . . She roused herself from the contemplation of his mouth, gave the towel a little jerk forward. He didn't take it. Silence but for the rain.

'You were limping,' she croaked at last.

Hal nodded without taking his eyes from her, still that ferociousness about him.

'When you rolled out of the way of my car that day, did you really hurt yourself?' she asked.

'Not stricken with conscience after all, are you, Stacey?'

'Am I responsible?' she insisted.

'A few bruises, that's all. I know how to fall.'

'It's a old injury, then?'

'A road accident. I was hit by a car a long time ago. It put me in hospital for five months.'

'Five months!' So long to be cooped up in a hospital room. For a man like Hal, it must have been hell. 'No wonder you were so furious! It must have been like history repeating itself.'

'I've had happier moments,' he admitted with a wry twist of his mouth.

Stacey bit her lip. 'I'm sorry I wasn't more—well, I'm sorry. And that crack about a phoney limp—I wish I hadn't said that.' With one elbow rested on the steering wheel, his big shoulders wedged sideways, he blocked out half the windscreen and the side window. She waited a little while but he said nothing. 'Well?' she prompted.

'Well what?'

'I just apologised to you. Aren't you going to say something?'

'Is it such a momentous occasion? You, apologising?'

She thought about it, following a bobbing yellow raincoat that seeped its colour down the windscreen. 'Yes,' she said, looking back at him. 'I hardly ever apologise.'

Hal laughed and took the towel from her at last, easing back in his seat to use it. 'I would have hired a brass band if you'd given me warning.' He rubbed at his hair until it stood straight up, then he flicked his comb through it.

'I accept your apology, Stacey Jamieson,' he said, starting the car.

'You haven't limped since that first day. What sets it off? Is it rainy weather?' she added, recalling that it had been raining early on the day he'd arrived at Jamieson House.

The Alfa slid on to the street. 'My leg gives me clear warning of rain—and trouble.' He glanced at her. 'Maybe you are partly responsible, after all.'

The week that followed was quite different from the first. Stacey caught up with her darkroom work, and went out on a baby portrait job for Coe's. Hal went along and helped her coochy-coo the infant into the laughing pose her mother desired. She tried out some black and white infra-red film in the Botanic Gardens and did a photo-session on the Harbour when they caught ferries back and forth while she photographed the foreshore and the water craft and the city. She put in some practice on the tennis court with the ball-machine, and coaxed Hal into playing with her. She was too good for him, but only because it wasn't his game and she'd had years of coaching and playing. He had superb reflexes and strength and a height advantage, and he whittled down her leads to a narrow margin in no time at all. 'Another couple of weeks and I'll have trouble winning a game off you!' she laughed.

'With a bit of luck the police will find our crank and I won't be here that long,' Hal replied, and the thought ran through Stacey's mind then that she hoped the police wouldn't find the crank. Which was crazy, stupid, when every now and then she remembered that someone might be watching, waiting to aim a gun at her or push her under a bus or use a knife . . . She'd remembered it one day in the city as they walked to the car, and she had to force herself to walk straight instead of pulling in her head and shrinking up small to make the tiniest possible target. Damn it, she thought fiercely, she wasn't going to let some cowardly writer of anonymous letters turn her into a turtle! But her mouth was dry and her nails dug into her palms, and she wondered if this was how an anxiety attack started. Hal took her hand then. Just that. Not a word. Took her hand and held it tight as they walked—and with the promise of his strength to augment her own, she discovered she had more than she thought.

They bickered, because Stacey was used to having her own way, and Hal came on strong and overruled her and usually won. It became a daily routine for them to compose rhymes about the presents, but they still couldn't come up with one about the Sedgwicks' lustres. Hal went with her to choose a birthday present for Alex. He tagged along when she bought her photographic supplies, and asked the kind of questions a photographer loves to answer. They ate Grace's lunches together. 'Join us for lunch, Grace,' Hal would say. 'Bring your nut cutlets and beansprouts in and sit with us.'

'None of your vegetarian jokes, if you please,' Grace would sniff, but the sparkle in her eyes belied the stern set of her mouth.

They jogged around the Jamieson House grounds together, sat in the library reading, not talking. Even not talking with Hal had a nice, companionable feel to it. When they did talk, Stacey wanted to know more about Cedar Hill and his brothers and sisters. 'I always wanted a sister or brother,' she said dreamily. 'When I was about six I used to pretend I had a brother. I used to hide inside the fireplace in the green drawing-room and talk to him about school and my dolls——'

'What was his name?' smiled Hal.

'I can't remember, isn't that terrible? He was so important to me and I can't remember what I called him.' Stacey frowned, disturbed more than the memory slip warranted. So many memory slips. So many things she'd forgotten, so much she'd never noticed.

Having Hal around to share so many ordinary things was the nearest she'd ever had to a brother. He treated her like a younger sister—abusing her frankly but without heat when she stepped on his toes. 'Brat,' he would say, or, 'What a little bitch you are,' or, 'Pipe down, kid,' but she thought there was a note of affection in it. Whether it was brotherly or not she could never be sure. But she knew she didn't feel like his sister. Not at all.

'I don't think much of this,' he said once about a photograph he'd seen her set up for the previous day. He always asked to see each batch of film she developed. 'But this one isn't too bad.'

Stacey felt a bit peeved. 'I can live with that opinion, seeing that all you know about photography is "say cheese" and press the button.'

'I tell you the truth as I see it,' he shrugged. There were no flowery compliments from Hal. Chris and her father always said, 'Marvellous, darling,' and 'Absolutely beautiful, pet,' to her pictures, and while she wished Hal would say he loved her work, she came to appreciate his honesty more. Chris's unconditional flattery had always somehow left her unsatisfied. Hal's criticism and his occasional, 'That's great!' she grew to value. She didn't show him the photographs of himself.

Fortunately, her mother was too tied up with party arrangements and her charity committees to notice the rapport between Stacey and her bodyguard. She and Brian relaxed a little as the days went by and there was no trouble.

'Looks like a hoax, after all,' her father said bracingly at dinner one night. 'Nothing's happened.'

Oh, but something had, Stacey thought. Something. She made excuses not to go out with Chris. She didn't ask herself why; she was curing herself of asking embarrassing questions.

'You said you were doing this job as a favour, Hal—why do you owe Dad a favour?' she asked one day as they ate lunch after a hectic doggie portrait sitting. The dog, an excitable Affenpinscher, had a pedigree as long as her much married and divorced mistress, and the combination had been wearying.

'She's a real—bitch!' Hal had muttered on leaving.

'Mrs Warburton or dear little Dolores?' Stacey had asked with a giggle. His black look encompassed Dolores and her owner.

'I just owe him, that's all,' he said. They sat on the

sand near rows of upturned boats and looked out at the waters of Watson's Bay, abob with masts. Seagulls wheeled and squealed in a winter-blue sky.

'I could always ask my father,' Stacey pointed out, taking off her shoes.

'Brat!' muttered Hal. He leaned back on his elbows and did a slow surveillance of the beach, the bay, the noisy seafood restaurant close by, before he unwrapped his sandwiches. His eyes were squinting against the silver glare of sun on water. 'I left the police force and joined Talisman, and I was doing pretty well,' he told her. 'Promoted to security on the boardroom floor, where I saw a lot of your father. I was able to avert some trouble with a VIP once, and he grew to trust me. Then I had that argument with a car and lost.' He bit off half a ham and salad sandwich, and Stacey waited impatiently for him to go on.

'Well?' she queried.

'I recovered, but couldn't pass the medical. All the Talisman security staff have to pass a medical, so I had to leave.'

'Were you sorry?'

He sent her an exasperated look. 'Of course I was sorry! I was twenty-three, in perfect health, about to compete in the world karate titles, working my way up towards becoming security chief for a multi-national company, and suddenly I was unemployed and walking with a stick.' He shook his head. 'I can't expect you to understand. You've never had to lose anything, have you, brat?'

'Only my self-respect,' she snapped, thinking of her humiliation when she found out she was under surveillance and too dim to notice. 'But then, we rich people don't feel things like that too deeply. I could always buy some more, right?'

His gaze rested thoughtfully on her a moment, then he looked out at the bay's sweetly swaying masts. 'The problem was, technically I wasn't covered by Talisman's insurance. The accident occurred off duty, which meant I was liable for all my own medical expenses. It didn't take too long to run through my savings. I had a beat-up Holden I'd restored, a partly paid off piece of land and a few thousand in savings. It was all gone within six weeks.'

'But surely medical insurance——'

'It didn't come anywhere near it. I had seven operations, specialist surgeons, physiotherapy, lab tests and five months of hospital care. For a time it looked as if I might lose my leg——' Hal rubbed a hand down his right thigh. 'It's not pretty, but it's functional. Skin grafts, muscle grafts, bone grafts—a couple of steel pins and plate.'

'What about the driver who hit you?' asked Stacey.

'That's where your father came in. The driver refused to admit responsibility—made out I was drunk—and he had a top lawyer and things looked set to drag on for years. Meanwhile, my parents were just about ready to sell their house to pay for my treatment.'

'Sell their *house* to pay hospital bills?' Stacey stared.

'Yes, Stacey,' he said in an overly patient kind of voice, 'it really does happen. But by chance your father found out how things were and pulled out all the stops—got me a top legal man and applied a bit of pressure here and there and let it be known that he was behind me. With the Jamieson name being bandied about I was saved from too much pestering about bills until damages were awarded. I came out of it with a bionic leg and more money than I'd ever seen in my life,' he said drily. 'Not an ideal exchange, to my mind, but then I guess that's why they call it compensation.

I went into partnership with a friend, Mick Yakubo, in the martial arts school, and later I bought Cedar Hill—and that's taken care of the money.'

'By chance, you said. What if Dad hadn't found out things were so bad and helped you—I mean, would you or your parents have asked for his help before they sold their house?'

'There's no pride stiffer than that of people who have little else. Our family would sell everything they own rather than ask anyone else to foot their bills.' He grimaced. 'Old-style working-class ethics. I'm grateful Brian stepped in—it meant I didn't have to bear the burden of my parents losing so much they'd worked so hard for.'

A family tragedy averted, and it had probably cost her father little effort, Stacey thought. It was unlikely he'd had to 'pull out all the stops'. A phone call here—a word with a lawyer, probably a member of the same club. There were a lot of people in high places keen to do him a personal favour. It didn't seem fair somehow that his casual interest, an instruction or two to a secretary, could be the difference between solvency and ruin to others. She felt vaguely guilty on behalf of those who never had to give a thought to survival.

'But then, you see, I owed Brian a favour. A big favour. I'm glad he called it in,' Hal said.

Stacey frowned up at the sky. 'When I nearly ran you over when you arrived, I bet you wished he'd asked you to do something more than just babysit a spoiled brat because of a couple of crank letters.'

Slowly he turned his head to her. 'Something more?'

'It's a bit trivial really, isn't it? Looking after me when it probably isn't really necessary—in return for saving your family from possible ruin. I mean, with your pride, you might feel it doesn't really even the score.' Stacey mulled it over for a second or two. 'But you shouldn't, you know. His scale of values might be different, but what you're doing for Dad is every bit as valuable to him as his favour was to you. There aren't many people a rich man can trust completely, when it comes right down to it.'

There was a long pause. A gull flapped down to a landing beside them, and Hal tossed it the crumbs from his sandwich wrapper. Within moments there were dozens of the birds—a jostling mass of soft grey and white feathers and bright black eyes and bills and black and vermilion legs and webbed feet. Stacey reached for her camera.

'There are times,' said Hal as she raised the Hasselblad and squinted, 'when I think you're not all bad, brat.'

'Oh, my! You don't know how much that means to me.' She clapped a hand to her heart. The seagulls took off and she turned her camera to the bay waters and adjusted the polarising filter.

'That'll be just another postcard view,' he warned, getting up to throw his lunch wrapper in a bin. 'Unless you include a bit of human interest.'

Stacey turned the lens on him. 'In that case, *you'll* have to do.'

Talk about human interest! She couldn't think of anything more human or interesting than Hal. 'Come on, Hal, stand over there and look natural,' she invited.

'Forget it,' he growled, but she advanced on him, camera raised, and he backed off, spreading a hand in front of his face. 'Come on, Stacey——'

She giggled, surprised and rather touched to discover that big, fearless Hal Stevens didn't like having his picture taken. 'Coward!' she taunted, edging him back and back until the inevitable happened. He stepped into the gently lapping bay waters. His shoes filled and his trouser ends soaked up the wetness. Stacey's laughter echoed out along the beach, over the water. She got the camera to her eye and caught everything—Hal's back-flung head and silent cursing, the glowering look he beamed at her while water squelched in his shoes. She moved around him in a cameraman's crouch, crooning encouragement between her giggles. 'Great, just great—give me that husky, outdoors quality. Terrific!' He yanked off his shoes and socks, rolled up his trousers. 'Bare feet! Provocative, earthy!' She wolf-whistled.

Hal stuffed his socks inside his shoes and tossed the lot on to the sand to advance purposefully on her. Filled with delicious apprehension, Stacey backed off as she recalled another joke and another expanse of water. 'Now, Hal—be a sport——' she pleaded, backing away, laughing, the breeze whipping her hair across her face. Eventually she turned and ran, her heart pounding crazily, her laughter breathless and carrying. She felt his hand close warmly around her arm, felt the solid presence of him close behind her, and she played the game and made a last struggle to evade him. She was ready and willing to be caught. She didn't expect to get away, but she did.

A little further on she stopped and looked around at him. Hal stood, hands on hips.

'You let me get away!' she accused, hiding her disappointment.

He just smiled and bent to pick up a shell. It was broken and he tossed it aside. Two more he picked up were similarly damaged. Stacey eased a partly buried shell from the sand. It was common enough, nicely curled along the edges with a few dominant stripes, but it was in one piece, only a tiny hole rendering it imperfect. She grinned at him. 'I've got a nose for finding shells.'

'Will you put it with that collection you keep in your bedroom?' he asked.

Stacey's face warmed a bit at the recollection of him in her room. 'No. I haven't added to it since I was a child——' And walking with Hal in that quiet curve of the bay, with the gulls gliding and the boats serene on the water, she told him about the days that always seemed sunny and the thrill of excavation and the magic of finding jewels in the sand.

She had the shell in her hand when they left, so she kept it. Later, she didn't know why, she put it with her collection.

CHAPTER FIVE

HE'D BEEN at this job a week too long, Hal thought as he followed Stacey into the department store. At the end of one week he'd more or less firmed on the image of Stacey Jamieson as a spoiled, selfish, frivolous kid with likable qualities. At the end of two he realised she was all those and much more. She had a heap of accomplishments that were pretty useless outside her own set—she knew about wines and food and she spoke French, as he found out when she introduced him to someone as a cousin. Before he could open his mouth, she added provocatively, 'But he only speaks French.' And she'd released a flood of French at him, ending on a questioning note to which he answered the only French word whose pronunciation he could risk, *'Oui.'* A finishing school in France had provided her with her excellent French, she told him later. She also spoke German and Italian. He'd always meant to learn a second language. 'I'm a cordon bleu cook and I play a little piano and saxophone,' she'd informed him. The saxophone was one of her jokes. She had a sense of fun and she had guts.

He knew she was often frightened, but she kept the lid on it. Other girls might have gone to pieces, but not Stacey. With help, she could be one hell of a woman. If someone dared winkle her out of her safe cocoon, away from Daddy and the boyfriend and the smothering effect of wealth, she could be everything a man could want. If someone dared.

79

Hal eyed her glossy light auburn hair and her straight back and her glorious backside. Moodily, he shoved his hands into his pockets. Forget it. You're not the some-one. You owe her father, remember, and persuading his little girl out into the real, harsh world would not be considered suitable repayment. Anyway, for all her doubts right now, she wouldn't really want to do any-thing about it. Stacey would continue to kid herself that she could live this life and have her freedom, too. Better that way. She might have guts, but it would take a lot for her to change things.

Stacey stopped suddenly, and he grabbed her by the waist to avoid tripping over her. For a moment she was close, all the scented sweetness of her hair whirling in his face, her perfume in his nostrils, her beautiful curves pressed back against him. I'm just here to protect the goods, he chanted silently. It was his mantra of late—just here to protect the goods. Her waist was small and the flare of her hips down to that fabulous rear almost irresistible. He should have kept his hands in his pockets. Stacey looked around and up at him, smiling, her green-blue eyes aglow.

'It's my old nanny—Marion Driesfeld!' And she was off, calling to a short, chubby woman hung with shopping bags. Hal lengthened his stride to keep up, used now to Stacey's impulsive changes of direction. Her nanny, had she said? He gave a snort of laughter. If he needed anything other than his debt to her old man to remind him of the void between himself and Stacey, this would do it. Girls who had nannies were definitely not of his world.

The women hugged. Marion Driesfeld was brown-haired and jolly. Years of dealing with children had stultified her adult conversation; she talked like the hostess of a pre-school children's show.

'And now, who is this?' she demanded brightly, fixing Hal with a curious eye. He felt he should have been labelled with his name in nice big lower-case letters.

'This is Hal Stevens,' Stacey smiled, and Hal waited to see if today he was to be a Spanish-speaking Mexican cousin, or something equally exotic and uncomfortable. But she said merely, 'Hal's a friend of mine,' with a slightly surprised look at him, as if the simple explanation had slipped out before she thought. He smiled, warmed. Friend? Did he feel like Stacey's friend? He was slightly surprised himself to discover that, all temptation aside, the answer was yes.

'How do you do, Ms Driesfeld.' He shook the nanny's hand.

'Oh no, not Ms,' she said stoutly. 'I'm *Miss* and proud of it. I shall call you Hal,' she added with an air of bestowing an honour upon him. 'What do you do, Hal?'

Hal felt like a kid at 'show and tell'. 'I'm in health,' he said seriously, much as some would say, 'I'm in oil,' and Marion Driesfeld apparently saw nothing odd about that. She nodded her approval, congratulated Stacey on her coming of age, thanked her for the party invitation which she'd had to refuse, and said that she had dispatched a gift in the mail. She then suggested they repair to the nearest coffee lounge for a cappuccino, and Stacey went along without a murmur. Here was one person who brooked no argument from the wilful Miss Jamieson, thought Hal, amused, as he followed them to the store's coffee shop. A child might grow up to question the authority of a parent, but nannies apparently retained their mystique.

Marion Driesfeld directed the seating arrangements and plumped herself down beamingly. She also ordered the coffee as if they were both mere children out for a treat. Then, a faint froth from her cappuccino decorating her upper lip, she reminisced about Stacey as a little girl.

'Such a starry-eyed little thing—she had no fear of the water or anything. I could never make her understand that there might be dangers. Do you know, she used to try to slide down the banisters of that monstrous staircase, and——' she gave an arch smile to Hal '—she won't like me saying so, but she was a terror for getting her gear off! If she was the least bit warm, off would come everything.'

'Good lord! Everything?' Hal murmured with a slanted look at Stacey. Her cheeks were pink and her eyes dared him to mention her latest unclothed episode. As Marion Driesfeld prattled on, Hal's mind wandered to moonlight and black lace and Stacey, naked and natural, twirling around to give him a heart-stopping view—leaning lovingly to touch her seashells with tender fingers. He watched her as she laughed at Nanny's less embarrassing recollections. Everything about her glowed—her eyes, her skin, her hair. Hal remembered the feel of that hair slipping through his fingers. Belatedly, he reminded himself that her glow was the bread and butter of a small army of hairdressers and beauticians.

'I remember how you loved those beach holidays,' Nanny Driesfeld chattered on.

Stacey propped her chin on her hand. 'Did it ever rain when we were at the beach?' she asked, her green-blue eyes intent, suddenly serious.

'Oh my, yes! One summer it rained non-stop for ten days, I remember.'

'I don't remember that . . . I don't remember any rain at all.'

That seemed to bother her, Hal thought. Stacey frowned.

'None of my children ever loved the beach as much as you,' Nanny went on. 'I said to Mrs Jamieson, we should buy sun-cream in bulk! You couldn't wait to get on to the sand every morning. Sometimes I had to be up at five to make sure I got there first.'

'First, Nanny?' Stacey shook her head, smiling.

'Yes, you know—to hide the "jewels" where you could find them. I'm sure you must have guessed when you were older.'

Coffee-cup half-way to her lips, Stacey looked stunned—her smile frozen, her eyes wide open.

'Oh my, yes, quite a challenge it was. I had to leave myself little markers so that I'd know where I'd hidden the latest ones. Sometimes I popped them in the sand and sometimes in a rock pool, although I gave that up because a little stray boy came along once and found one I'd planted in a rock pool before I could give you a nudge in the right direction. My, I was so annoyed!' She drank some more cappuccino, added to her moustache. 'You were so happy, finding such lovely jewels! You'd rush up to your mother, and your father, too, when he could get away from work to come down, and show them your latest find. So excited, so pleased with yourself——'

'Where did they come from? asked Stacey, meeting Hal's eyes over the rim of her coffee-cup, only to look away quickly. He concentrated on her as Nanny went on.

'Your father bought them from a collector. The poor man hated parting with them, but he needed the money . . . they were really quite valuable as a collection. I don't suppose you've still got them?'

Yes, Stacey still had them.

'Oh, well, then you probably know by now that some of them are quite rare. When you're a child you only care that they're pretty, but you'd realise now that they're from all over the world.'

Yes, of course, Stacey realised that.

'He was a nice man. I had a bit of a chat with him when he brought them to the house. His wife was very sick, and he had to sell things to pay all the bills . . . such a shame . . .' The coffee-break might have gone on for hours, but that Nanny had an appointment. She kissed Stacey soundly and shook Hal's hand, and was gone in a rustle of shopping bags. Stacey was silent as they drove home. Silent as Hal used the remote control and opened the Jamieson House gate.

'*Did* you know the shells were collector's items?' asked Hal, after several glances at her rigid profile.

Her laugh was high and scratchy. 'Well, of *course* I knew! Only an idiot would keep those shells all this time and not find out their proper names. I mean,' she shrugged one shoulder, 'at first I didn't know because I was naïve enough to think I'd just been luckier than my friends who only ever found periwinkles and—ordinary things like that.' Again the high-pitched laugh. 'People used to give me funny looks when I showed them my shells and I told them where I found them, so of course I knew there was something odd about it.' A hectic pause. 'I remember showing them to my teacher, Miss Markham, when I was about seven, and she said, "Those are rare shells to find on the east coast of Australia." Only a fool would go on thinking that some trick of tide or nature had delivered a whole collection of rare shells to her feet.' Another pause. 'Only a blazing *nitwit* would never catch on that they'd been planted for her to find and she'd been guided right to them!' Her face was suffused with colour. Hal reached out for her hand, but she snatched it away as the car purred to a stop in the garage forecourt. Then she leapt out and slammed the door mightily behind her, strutting off into the shadowed depths of the garages. They were empty but for the green Jaguar. Her footsteps echoed.

'Stacey!' called Hal, hastily turning off the ignition and hurrying after her. He cursed under his breath, nervous whenever she shot out of his sight like this. Not that it was likely anything would happen on her own home ground, but still—— A dull thud from Alex's House of Stoush turned him in that direction, and he burst in, a hand inside his jacket. The punchbag was swinging. Stacey was dragging on a boxing glove. She flung away from him as if to hide her face.

'Go away!' she yelled, and let fly with a punch at the bag. Her unfastened glove fell off.

'Here.' Hal got to it first and picked it up. 'I'll fasten them for you.'

'Just leave me alone!' Stacey belted the bag again with her bare hand. Grimacing, she put her burned knuckles to her mouth. The bag bucked sideways and caught Hal a mild blow on the ribs. He grabbed her wrist and shoved the glove over her hand, then swiftly tied both gloves and stepped out of range. She threw a punch at the bag and it slewed back and knocked her off her feet. That made twice in an hour. Nanny had bowled her over, metaphorically speaking, and now she was down, literally. Hal leaned over her like a referee, sympathetic but amused all the same. He began a countdown. 'One—two—three——'

On five, she jumped to her feet and pelted her fists overarm at the bag, which shuddered and swung out of reach so that every alternate blow was a miss. Stepping behind the bag, Hal put his arms around it and his weight behind it to keep it steady. 'Don't pound at it like a little girl throwing a tantrum,' he taunted. 'Keep your wrist up, straighten your arm, get your body behind the punch.'

Stacey rammed her fist into it and the resounding

'thwack' of it and Hal's surprised jolt as he absorbed
the shock appeared to satisfy her. A left and a right and
another right. She danced on her toes the way Alex did
and punched until she panted, muttering now and then,
'I found them *all* by myself. Ha!' and 'Idiot!' and
'Dimwit!' At last she wrapped both arms about the bag
and sagged against it. Eyes closed, she rested her face
against the canvas, not so very far from his own. Hal
felt the thrust of her weight against him and spread his
feet a little. His arms were around the canvas bag, as
were hers. If it wasn't for the dangling bolster they
would be holding each other, he thought, feeling the
heave of her body through the padded barrier.

'Stacey, sweetheart,' he said softly, raising a hand to
brush her hair from her damp brow. Her eyes opened.
Their colour was intensified by a film of tears. Such
hurt he saw there, such humiliation and self-derision
and self-doubt. His hand curved along the side of her
face, and suddenly her lips trembled and the tears
poured hotly down, then she wrenched herself away and
ran to the house, batting at her eyes with her gloved
hands. Half-way up the main staircase she managed to
tear one glove off and tossed it aside without looking.
Hal paused a moment in his pursuit to pick it up, raising
his eyes to watch Stacey's flight up to the gallery. Wryly
he turned the boxing glove over in his hand. A sort of
Cinderella in reverse, he thought. Then he followed her.

Stacey was by her glass display case when she heard him
come in. Her mind was full of visions of herself, proud
and cockily sure, showing her collection off to everyone. She thought of Miss Markham's odd expression
which she had delightedly thought was awe, but was
more likely pity and contempt for the little girl who had
everything, even rare seashells salted on the seashore for

her. 'She shall have seashells on the seashore,' she said
bitterly out loud. Oh, very funny! Miss Markham had
played the game. She hadn't let on what she must have
guessed—that it was all a giant, loving, indulgent hoax.
How many other people might have allowed her to
believe in her 'achievement'? Stacey wondered. Not that
it mattered. She had been so certain of her cleverness
that she had never picked up the clues offered her by not
so indulgent parties. She turned as Hal came to stand
beside her. Now she knew why his expression had
always bothered her. It was like Miss Markham's. Hal
had felt pity and contempt for her from the start—as
she romped about taking photographs and having dress
fittings and thinking about her party while other people
took responsibility for her safety, and she, too self-
absorbed even to read the clues, remained blissfully
unaware.

Staring at her shells, she burned. All the times she'd
boasted. All the times she'd blithely ignored the
comments that should have told her this was all a sham.
Everything she'd ever done or won suddenly carried a
question mark. Were these the only jewels buried in the
sand for her to find? Or had she been obediently
allowing herself to be led all these years to what was
already planted for her? Like Chris. Chris with his
impeccable background, his 'blue' blood that Hal had
mentioned, his parents who had old money and were
Friends of the Opera and wouldn't say no to a daughter-
in-law not quite up to scratch as far as lineage went, so
long as she'd been carefully brought up. Properly
finished. Properly guided. Mouldable. Rich.

'Damn, *damn!*' she yelled, and swept an arm across
the top, then the middle shelf and the lowermost.
Seashells sprayed like spiked shrapnel. Stacey covered
her face with her hands, the bare one and the leather-

gloved one, and howled. When Hal pulled her into his arms, she clutched at him. 'I always thought I found them . . . I always thought I was so clever, so smart. I—I—they were special. I stopped playing with dolls when I was ten—I threw out my teddy bear before that—but I always kept them. And it was all a phoney. *I'm* a phoney!'

'Ssssh!' Hal rocked a little from side to side, cradling her. She was glad he didn't tell her that she was wrong and everything would be all right. She was glad he didn't attempt to give her a solution. Only she could work it out. All she needed was a shoulder to cry on, and she took his offer gratefully and cried on his. He wrapped his arms around her and leaned his cheek against the top of her head, rubbing gently. Her tears flooded on to his shirt until her sobs turned to sniffs.

'Ease up,' murmured Hal, tipping her face up. He smoothed away the moisture on her cheeks and dropped a kiss on her nose. Stacey swallowed hard, staring at him as his eyes wandered over her. He stroked her hair, then smiled encouragingly and dropped another light kiss on her lips this time. A light, light kiss meant to comfort. A light, light kiss that lingered a moment too long for comfort. Her nerve-ends were shrieking the news and there were other signals in the air. Stacey looked into warm brown eyes and was struck with a breathlessness that had nothing to do with her crying jag. Again he kissed her, lightly, lingering longer. Her lips parted to match his, and if there had been any shred of comfort left it vanished now in a languorous, delicious exploration that escalated as fast as her heart-rate. Hal's arms slid down until he was holding her by the waist, as if he meant to push her away.

'Tell me to get the hell out of here,' he growled, his mouth seeking the curve of her neck even as he moved her body out of contact with his.

'Get the hell out of here,' she repeated, but it sounded more like an invitation. He kissed her once, twice on the neck, nuzzled inside her collar to her shoulder, and all this while, inexorably, he put her at arm's length. Stacey clutched at him, her hands sliding reluctantly from his shoulders to his chest, then losing contact altogether, falling to her sides.

Hal released her, took a huge breath that swelled his chest. He let it out with a wry, 'Whew!' and ran a hand distractedly through his hair. 'That's the last time I let you cry on *my* shoulder,' he said, as if those kisses were all her doing. Stacey flushed.

'So sorry! Did I take advantage of you?' she snipped, waving one hand. It was the one still encased in the boxing glove, and she did a double-take at the sight of the battered brown leather. She'd forgotten about that. Turning her back on him, she pulled at it, anxious to be rid of it and him.

'Here.' He took her by the shoulders, spun her around and removed the glove, then collected the other one and the gun which was on the dressing-table. He must have removed his weapon as he came in. How very thoughtful of him! 'Maybe you were anticipating a clinch,' she drawled, 'and a good bodyguard doesn't tote a gun when he gets his client in a clinch.'

'My mistake,' he said drily, swinging the boxing gloves, watching them. 'My defences were sloppy. Too long out of the arena, I suppose.'

Stacey caught her breath. So he'd been isolated from his social life for a couple of weeks and any woman would have tempted him—was that what he was saying?

'Get the hell out of here!' she commanded.

'That's better, sweetheart,' he approved. 'Much more conviction——'

He opened the door sharply and shut it as fast behind him as she hurled a hairbrush at him. It bounced off the door and she sat down on a stool and stared at it, then at her scattered shells. Poor little rich girl, she thought. She'd always wondered what they meant by that.

To enter the Jamieson House ballroom on the night of Stacey's twenty-first birthday celebration was to step back in time. The columned, gilt-trimmed walls were garlanded in the Edwardian manner with tiny roses and orchids and trailing plants. On the tables, more orchids of cream and pink and velvety burgundy, this last to match the high-backed, brocaded chairs. There was silver to catch the light and send it raying upwards— silver ice buckets and cutlery and candelabra. There was crystal, diamond-bright: goblets and finger bowls and huge, faceted punchbowls. Chandeliers and champagne. Amber floor with the satiny patina of age. Lustrous-bodied violins and the bold brass of cornets and coiled French horns on the orchestra dais. Musicians in the ageless black and white of evening dress.

Later there would be a rock band which would play until morning or until the guests dropped, whichever came first. In the meantime there was the formal business of greeting guests and using her rhymes to remember names and match them to the gifts now displayed on the massive mahogany table. Stacey stood for an hour and a half, smiling, shaking hands, kissing cheeks, phrasing her thanks just right. She could make it as a politician, she thought, glancing over at Hal who, along with a host of other security people, was close by. He looked superb. The finesse of the dinner jacket and frilled shirt was a counterpoint to his rough-finished cheekbones, his ruged jaw and the cool, watchful eyes.

They swung around to her now, those eyes. He gave a polite, reassuring smile—bodyguard to client. 'Everything's OK—don't worry,' that sort of smile. The only kind he seemed to have for her tonight. It only altered when he heard her greet the Sedgwicks. They never had settled on a rhyme for the Sedgwicks' gift, but so many outrageous attempts had locked them and the lustres together in Stacey's memory for ever. Hal's smile, then, was briefly genuine as they silently shared their amusement.

Since that scene in her room yesterday he had withdrawn something from her—a little of his warmth, his friendship. In a small way he had let her into his life, but the door was pleasantly slammed shut the moment he ducked out of her room. Stacey, smarting from greater hurts, was nevertheless stung by the knowledge that, after all, she was nothing more to Hal than a client. He had probably used his humour and his charm in the past to keep clients relaxed—even entertained. She knew she should be grateful to him. The past two weeks could have been nerve-racking had he been some stolid, insensitive clod with no conversation, no sense of fun to play along with her jokes. She *was* grateful to him, but she was peeved, too. She sent him a brilliant smile in response, just to show him that she didn't give a damn about him or about the crank who might or might not attempt to make trouble tonight.

The house had been searched this evening, all the staff lined up and checked against their identification. There were rumbles among the staff of the catering firm who had been here many times before. The chefs, of course, were cleared separately, discreetly, deferentially. No one in their right mind would subject chefs to such an indignity as a line-up just before they prepared the food for a gala occasion.

Bow-tied security men were everywhere. There was even one in the orchestra, plaintively wielding maracas. Photographers too were everywhere, darting about to catch Sydney's élite, rich or famous at play.

Stacey posed with her parents, with Chris, with Chris's parents, with old schoolfriends. Later there were toasts to her future, as she sat at the main table, flanked by Chris and her father. The toasts were preceded by speeches and coy references to her baldness as a baby, her temperament as a teenager, her beauty as a woman. The reminiscences fell flatly on Stacey's ears; it was as if they were talking about someone else. She was no longer sure just who Stacey Jamieson was. Perhaps she was a fabrication. A well-put-together model crafted according to her parents' blueprints. She delivered a speech of thanks to all these people, very few of whom were here to celebrate Stacey Jamieson's birthday. This party was a triumphant exercise in public relations for her father, she thought bitterly. Oh, certainly he wanted her to enjoy it, but the prime intention was to impress, to leave his mark on society. And the guests were here because it was a good idea to be seen as friends of the Talisman boss. Like the opera first-night audiences, this gathering was full of pragmatists. Guiltily, she made some exceptions. This bitterness was over-reaction. She smiled brilliantly and acted the role of delighted heiress come-of-age because, no matter what, she loved her parents, and this night meant so much to them.

The act became easier with a few glasses of champagne to bolster her. She laughed and danced, and people nudged each other and speculated on how soon the engagement with young Holdsworth would be announced. It could even be tonight. She's worth a mint, of course. Now that she's twenty-one, she gets a cool million settled on her straight away—but with strings, naturally. Naturally! Jamieson was too fly to let a fortune-hunter get his hands on his money. He came from nowhere himself, you know. No background, none at all. Rumour has it he used to have a trucking business. Trucking? Yes. Well—hmm. Those days are over, wouldn't you say?

She was going to have to leave. Leave this house, this life. Stacey whirled around the floor with Chris, her attitude all gaiety, all celebration. If she hadn't been such a late developer she would have seen what was happening sooner and gone her own way before this. The knowledge settled in her heart like a cold, small pebble. Leaving wasn't going to be easy on any of them.

She drank some more champagne and went up on to the bandstand to join the orchestra. The bandleader listened to her request and the tenor saxophonist smilingly handed over his instrument to her. Stacey looked for Hal as she played an average version of 'Smoke Gets in Your Eyes', with the orchestra obligingly following her erratic rhythm. If you paid enough you could even play lousy saxophone with a bandstand full of highly trained musicians, Stacey thought, hoping she would be able to keep up the act until the night was over. She finished playing and bowed to the loud applause she didn't deserve. The story of my life, she thought, laughing and mock-curtseying. Taking bows for things I don't deserve. She bestowed a kiss upon the saxophonist as she gave back his instrument. A true spoiled rich brat, he must be thinking—but what the hell, the pay's good.

She spotted Hal at last, before she alighted from the stage in the role of frivolous heiress. He was by the doors, one shoulder against the wall, his arms crossed over his chest. When her eyes met his, he gave a mocking little incline of his head, so slight that most people would have missed it. It said heaps to Stacey. It said that her act was wildly successful.

It took a while to actually make it to his side, but she did, spilling a little champagne from her glass as she went. That was all right. She was the party girl, the guest of honour. If she spilled her drink—so what? 'You didn't believe I really *could* play the saxophone, did you?' she laughed.

'You're right, I didn't.'

'I was good, wasn't I?' she bubbled. The cold pebble in her heart was a decent-sized rock now. 'Everyone thought I was terrific.'

Hal's mouth twisted. 'Of course.' He lowered his voice. 'You're drinking too much, even for one of your set.'

Gaily, she laughed. 'No, no—I'm spilling most of it, Hal darling.' She stretched her hand out sideways and the empty glass was removed immediately by a waiter. 'Come and dance with me?' She held out a hand to Hal.

'I'm on duty,' he replied disinterestedly, glancing around at the guests. There were some curious looks from those nearby.

'Don't be stuffy, Hal! Just one dance,' she pleaded. Just one dance. It was suddenly important. She'd danced with so many others tonight, and it had meant nothing at all. One dance with Hal, that would be special, something to remember. Her false vivacity fled for the moment. 'Please, Hal——' she said softly.

'There are plenty of men here to dance with, Stacey.'

'I don't want to dance with them, I want to dance with you.'

'Another novelty?' he said with a short laugh. 'Like playing sax with the orchestra? A dance with your bodyguard—forget it. I wasn't hired as a dancing partner.' Brown eyes snapping, he gave her a parting smile for the benefit of onlookers, and slowly turned away, as if his attention had drifted elsewhere. He was angry! Stacey registered the fact in astonishment. What did *he* have to be angry about? He hadn't had the rug pulled out from under him. *He* hadn't had to see his image of himself torn into a thousand little pieces. She caught up with him, linking her arm determinedly through his, smiling inanely for the onlookers, wiggling her fingers at a schoolfriend who rolled her eyes at Hal and mouthed, 'Who is *that?*'

'I want to talk to you.'

'You have guests, Stacey,' he reminded her, and removed her hand from his arm. He'd done that on the very first day. He was the only man who had ever wanted her to *stop* touching him. She felt terribly hurt by it, terribly lonely suddenly here in this ballroom full of people speaking her name, wishing her well. And when she was hurt, anger was never far away.

'I have to get out of here for a few minutes. I'm going into the conservatory, and as you *are* my bodyguard I expect you to come, too!' she hissed through a full-scale PR smile.

'Brat! There are plenty of other guards about. Les Howison, for instance. If you want to flounce off to look at the orchids you can do it with Les. His grammar isn't good, but he's a dependable man,' Hal said sarcastically.

Stacey gave him her sweetest *ingénue* smile. 'Oh, but I can easily lose darling, plodding Les or any of the others. They don't know how devious I can be.' She had him, she knew, when his teeth ground together and the frills of his dress shirt heaved. He fell back a pace or two, and Stacey began the long, diplomatic process of traversing the ballroom to duck out of the side door and along the passage that led to the conservatory's internal

door. Hal signalled the other guards who had discreetly
followed, to wait outside, and went in with Stacey.

Hot, moist air hit them. There were some ground-
level spotlights glowing, silhouetting palm fringes and
slender stems, spiky carnation foliage, trellised
tomatoes and the jungle of orchids, long knife leaves
and graceful flower bracts rising from them, black and
oriental against the pale gold light. Through the faceted
bronze glass was a sky full of stars. The orchestra was
playing a Billy Joel number. It was faint, elusive, like
music from a dream. Stacey turned around, while Hal
waited, watching her, frowning. She had had some
vague notion of confiding in him, telling him that she'd
decided to cut loose from the life he despised. Even
some idea of asking his advice. But, now that they were
alone, she was inhibited. She turned away from him
again suddenly, so that the skirt of her French taffeta
dress belled and rustled. She walked along to the
orchids. 'This one was a birthday gift from my god-
father,' she said brightly, touching a bract of the perfect
blooms. 'He bred this one for me . . . it's a type of
slipper orchid. I wonder if he'll call it Cypripedium
Stacey or something——' she laughed.

'Will this—whim of yours take long?' asked Hal,
walking along to her on the fine gravel walkway.
Begonias and cyclamen swayed at his passing. Pink and
pale lilac flowers bobbed on shadowed invisible stems.

'I just wanted to be alone with you, to—to——' She
dried up, suddenly near to tears, lost.

'To what?' He stood close to her. 'You're not usually
backward in saying what you want. What is it?'

'I—Hal, I——' She swayed towards him, and what
she wanted was there in her eyes. He stood very still. No
one could stand more still than Hal when he wanted,
like a sculptor's roughcast figure.

'Well, why not?' he mocked. 'It *is* your birthday, isn't it?' He stepped in close, caught her by the waist, pulled her none too gently to him. 'Let's get it over with before you're missed, hmm?' His mouth came down on hers with the force of the simmering anger in him, his arms swept around her, swamping her with his strength. her head dropped back under his pressure, and he thrust a hand into her hair to hold her where he wanted. Yet Stacey sensed it was all a sham, that he was working hard to keep his anger burning for some reason of his own, and she stayed still and held him, feeling the tension in him. For a man bent on getting it over with he was in no hurry. His kiss softened, lingered, wandered, across her cheek, down to her neck. The orchestra played dream music in some far-off place, and the dizzying scent of orchids hung in the hot, moist air. Hal kissed her shoulder, curved his hands to her ribs and slid them up until her breasts were framed within the stretch of his thumbs and fingers. Stacey gasped. Someone had turned the heating up, way up. Wildly she kissed him, twisting pleasurably in his arms, loving the way he touched her, making all the birthday wishes that had eluded her when she had cut her cake. I wish . . . I wish . . . Hal took her arms, removed them from about his neck and stepped back. He was always doing that. Always.

'Happy birthday, brat,' he said huskily. 'I'm going. If you don't care to come now, I'll send in our two friends who are waiting out there to watch over you.'

He turned around and was four paces away before Stacey caught him up. 'Hal!' She touched his arm, and the wall of the conservatory exploded.

CHAPTER SIX

STUPIDLY, as she fell back, Stacey thought the second was a direct consequence of the first. 'But I hardly touched you,' she protested as Hal whirled about and lunged to the ground with her, covering her with his body, his hand cupped over her face. The blast rocked the ground they lay upon, lit up the night. Glass shattered, tinkled, pots thudded to the ground. One broke close beside them. Stacey felt the brush of leaves and smelled the moist, spilled earth. The music stopped, voices rose, the sustained note of a woman's scream hung thinly in the crackling aftermath—her mother, Stacey thought, stunned, as she heard her name called from a long way off and the thud of feet rushing up and down the conservatory's walkways. Her body trembled, wouldn't stop. 'Hal—oh, Hal!' she cried, great gasping sobs tearing at her. Her hands patted at his big body lying so protectively over hers. He was so still. No one could be more still than Hal when he wanted. 'Don't be hurt . . . please, please be all right——'

He took in a huge breath, and the expansion of his ribs hurt hers. She must be bruised, she supposed vaguely, maybe she'd broken something . . . but her tears fell in relief that he was moving.

'All my fault. Shouldn't have come out here,' he murmured in her ear. 'Shouldn't have let you have your way, you spoiled brat.'

The two guards found them at last, and a babble of voices reached them as Hal carefully rose to his knees and lifted Stacey up.

'Any pain around your ribs?' he asked. But Stacey just shook her head, her eyes fixed on the blood running from the side of his neck.

'You're bleeding,' she said, and he lifted his hand to his face in a reflex gesture. Stacey caught his wrist and stared at the back of his hand. It was studded with glittering slivers of glass, some buried deep, others so precariously attached to his skin that they trembled, glittered like some wickedly beautiful fragments of a chandelier. Thin streams of blood ran down his hand into the white cuff of his evening shirt. 'You're hurt—you're hurt——' she babbled, shaking.

Then her father was there and Hal was not. Her mother came, anguished and muttering, 'Thank God, thank God,' over and over and patting Stacey's arms and face to reassure herself that she was unharmed. Brian Jamieson bellowed orders, and suddenly she was out of the conservatory with a coat around her shoulders. It was then she remembered that Hal's hand, spiked with glass splinters, had been the one shielding her face. Her shaking grew worse and she looked around for Hal to thank him, but he wasn't there.

'Sent him to the hospital. He's all right,' her father told her when she pestered to know where he was. Stacey herself was tended by their guest, Dr Dalkeith, who was professionally soothing. 'Doc Dalkeith,' chanted Stacey, giggling, 'you're a honey—for making like the Easter bunny.' Dr Dalkeith examined Stacey's head again. 'Eh—what's up, Doc?' she said *à la* Bugs Bunny. Scratches, bruises and shock, the doctor said, but a head X-ray might be advisable. Her levity vanished. 'I'm all right—honestly. Just talking nonsense to stop myself shaking.'

Alex turned up, ashen-faced. He took her hand in his

and patted it fiercely, saying, 'I'm sorry, girl, I'm sorry.' Everyone was saying things twice, she thought. Alex had intercepted a man running from the house, but he hadn't been able to hold him.

Fire-extinguishers hissed, police sirens wailed and the last, hardy society photographers who had stayed to the bitter end on the offchance of some pics of drunken VIP revellers slipped past in the pandemonium to photograph a newsman's dream—shattered glass, singed hot-house plants, gawping society matrons and politicians, a dirty, distraught heiress, and the crowning touch of five top-line rock stars arriving for their gig in tight trousers and light make-up, only to find they'd been upstaged.

'Stacey Jamieson, after her twenty-first birthday party which culminated in a bomb blast. Miss Jamieson suffered cuts and bruising——' 'Halden Stevens, a security employee, was injured by flying glass.' 'Members of rock group "The Fabled Few" booked to play at the party. "As a gig, it turned out a real blast," lead guitarist Ralphie Summers quipped.'

The party that would have dominated the social pages dominated the front page instead.

They moved out to a hotel while the house was combed for any further devices, and then they moved back in. Brian Jamieson was both anxious and furious that he'd been made to look such a fool. Nothing was actually said, there was no need. But there was a general accusatory silence that said plainly that his responsibility as a host had been to ensure the safety of his guests, and it was only sheer luck that there had not been wholesale carnage.

'Just exactly what were you doing out there, anyway? her father demanded of Stacey the next day. 'What was

Hal thinking of to let you into the conservatory, for God's sake?'

'It wasn't a case of him *letting* me,' she said sharply. 'I needed a break from the party and wanted to look at the orchid Uncle Malcolm gave me. Naturally, Hal went along—and a good thing he did.'

'He shouldn't have let you anywhere near the place,' her father said obstinately. Frustrated that all his money and power had not prevented the incident, and so far had not tracked down the culprit, who was known now to be one of the catering staff, Brian Jamieson was looking around to pin some blame wherever he could.

'I would have gone regardless, and he knew it. He saved my face. The normal reaction when bits of glass are being hurled into you is to flinch, and if he'd flinched that glass would have been in my face instead of his hand.' Grudgingly, her father allowed that. To her questions about Hal's health he merely said, 'He's all right. He won't be coming back for a few days. If we can find the son of a bitch who did this, he won't have to come back at all.'

No more Hal? Stacey found that depressing. She hadn't even said goodbye or thank you. Perhaps she would phone him . . .

'If Alex had been a bit quicker on his feet we would have had the bastard.' Her father's eyes narrowed against his cigar smoke. 'Alex is getting past it.'

Stacey sat up in alarm. 'You wouldn't—you're not thinking of replacing him?'

'An ex-boxer around the place seemed like good security at one time, but he's too old and too slow.'

'If Alex goes, so will Grace,' she protested.

'There are other housekeepers, pet.' Her father patted her hand, misreading her concern entirely. She was thinking about the Warmans, who had made their home here—to be dismissed would be like being cut off from family. But surely this was over-reaction on her father's part? When the fuss had died down he would realise he couldn't part with Alex and Grace.

Days passed and the culprit was still at large. Stacey wrote thank-you notes and tried to show some interest in the proofs of the party photographs—the pre-bomb photographs, that was. Hal showed up again, bandages on his hand, a plaster on his neck, but Stacey's pleasure at his return was dampened by his grim, uncommunicative manner. Her thanks for saving her from scarring were accepted brusquely. However heroic his actions had been, her father still believed he'd been derelict in his duty by allowing her out of the ballroom, and had obviously relayed that dissatisfaction to Hal. It occurred to Stacey, too, that Hal's own business must be suffering as this job dragged on, but his pride would prevent him walking out on it when he felt he owed the favour to her father.

The strain in the house was unbearable. Alex, humiliated over his inability to catch and hold the culprit, and in disfavour with Brian Jamieson, was drawn and haggard. His birthday celebration was far from jolly.

'Your stars say things will get worse before they get better, girl,' he said dolefully to Stacey.

Grace, resenting the blame being heaped on her husband's head, was withdrawn, her lean, vegetarian build sharpened to an Olive Oyl angularity. The food was awful. Clare Jamieson consoled herself with the Russian composers at the grand piano, while Brian was tense and edgy, the pages of his financial papers opening and shutting like the jaws of some fiscal monster.

Stacey found herself virtually a prisoner. Two beefy

escorts and Hal went everywhere with her. Her every move was regimented, her photography excursions banned on the grounds that they were unnecessarily dangerous. Several commissions were also cancelled arbitrarily, and without the solace of her work Stacey was stuck with tennis practice, workouts in Alex's House of Stoush, walks in the garden and jogging with Hal, which offered little pleasure when the beefy ones jogged along, too. When she went to lunch with those friends brave enough to risk her company, the heavies were there waiting to march her to her car. Her parents were shocked at the idea of any loosening of this military-style security. When she complained morosely to Chris, who called every night, he seemed surprised. 'You should be glad your father's taking such good care of you. I'll call around tomorrow again.'

'Do they search you before you're allowed in to visit the prisoner?' she asked scathingly.

'Now, Stacey, don't be silly. It's for your own good.'

'How long is this going to go on?' she demanded of her father.

'Until we find the person responsible.'

'But it could take weeks—months!' she cried, horrified.

'Whatever it takes,' said her father, hugging her but turning a deaf ear to her protests.

It took two weeks. Stacey sat in a courtroom and stared at the thin, small man who had made such a mark on her life. He drank, they said. His wife had left him and he had no family, they said. His car had been repossessed. Her eyes met his and she could see only tiredness, hopelessness, none of the fanaticism or hatred she'd expected from one who had written threatening letters and smuggled a home-made bomb into the house in the paraphernalia of the head chef. Somehow she'd been sure she would recognise the person responsible. Somewhere she would have seen him—somehow she must have slighted him without know-

ing, hurt him, and he had hit back. But though he had
been to the house several times with the catering firm, she
had never seen him. He was a stranger, an ordinary little
man with little, who hated those with much, but whose
hatred didn't show. Stacey found that frightening. Had he
raved and spewed out anger and reproach she could have
handled it and eventually put it aside. But that inoffensive
little man, so quiet, his spine bowed in chronic defeat
having made his one statement to the world, she would
remember always. As she left the courtroom her legs
shook. She was angry for the anxiety he'd caused her
parents, relieved that it was all over, but most of all she felt
a deep, terrible sadness for the man. And, paradoxically, a
little guilt for being who she was, with her nice, comfortable life.

So an ordinary little man was deprived of his freedom
and she was given hers back. Or so she thought.

There were arguments when she said she was leaving
home to set up on her own. Recrimination: 'We thought
you were happy here'. Amazement: 'What on earth do
you have to gain by moving?' Soothers: 'You've been
under a lot of stress. Let's think about it a while——'
Counter offers: 'We'll give you an entire wing of the house
to yourself, and how about a nice cruise somewhere?'
Then when she persisted, the arguments stopped. 'You
must do what you want, pet,' her father said. Stacey began
looking at properties, searching for a small terrace house
or unit to buy now that she had her trust money. But then,
when she found the perfect place, it was suddenly
withdrawn from sale, and there was a legal hiccup about
her money which limited her access to it. An appeal to her
father for a loan to buy another property met with the
surprising information that all his ready money was tied
up, but if she just waited a month . . . she saw it then.
Strings were still being pulled. The scare had turned her

father's passion for security into an obsession. When she discovered that a man tailed her everywhere she went, even now that the danger was past, she flew into a rage. Her father was loving, patient. He patted her hand. 'Humour your old dad,' he said. 'I don't want anything to happen to you.'

But she did want things to happen to her. She thought of Hal, whose job had been completed with the apprehension of the little man. It was tempting to go to see him. She even drove past his martial arts school one day, wondering what he would say if she went in. But she kept driving, remembering his casual farewell on the day the man was caught.

'It's been interesting,' he'd said, and there was a note of finality about that that stopped Stacey saying anything more. All over, finished, he seemed to be saying. It's been interesting. It was the kind of thing you said to a date you never intended dating again. The kind of thing you said when the truth would be too unkind and you couldn't bring yourself to tell a total lie. Interesting. No, she couldn't chase a man who summed up their odd, brief relationship as 'interesting'. Nevertheless, it went against the grain to stay away from Hal. There never had been anything she wanted to do that she hadn't done—anything that she wanted that she hadn't had. Except her freedom. It was not a case of her having her freedom back now that the threats had been removed. She'd never had it. If she wanted it she would have to take it before her resolution was crushed beneath the weight of her parents' determination to keep her safe until she was ransomed off to someone like Chris.

It wasn't easy, but she did it. Her departure lacked drama, for she had to pretend she was driving over to Chris's house for dinenr. The date was real and she felt bad about it. Poor Chris, she thought sadly. He was as much a prisoner of his family's conservative expansionism as she was of her family's ambition. There were lots of ways of being held to ransom.

Her car boot was stuffed with clothes smuggled out over days in shopping bags and her camera accessories bag. Her photographic equipment filled the car, but that would not draw comment, as it frequently did so when she did a portrait sitting. She just hoped no one would think it odd that she took it to Chris's house. Her father was at the office when she left. Her mother had friends in, and Stacey badly wanted to hug her, but couldn't. Instead, she smiled and said what she always said before she thought. 'I won't be late.' But she would be, and her mother would be so worried, even when she'd read the letter Stacey had left in her bedroom. There were several letters—one for her parents, one for Chris, one for the Warmans. She'd posted some to her friends, saying she was going overseas indefinitely.

It nearly killed her to be supremely casual when she knew she wasn't coming back. 'See you later,' she said to Grace as the housekeeper's angular form bent over a batch of dinner rolls Stacey would never sample. In the garage she threw a mock punch at Alex, and tossed her shoulder-bag and a coat on to the crowded front seat of the Alfa.

'A pansy punch,' scoffed Alex, and she quoted along with him as she started the car, 'Got to keep that wrist up, girl!'

She would need to keep more than her wrist up, Stacey thought as she drove down past the silky oaks that would soon bear spring green, past the banked azaleas yet to bloom and along the Alice-in-Wonderland cut-outs of the cypress trees on the circular drive. Mr Jaswinsky wheeled his barrow out of harm's way and she waved, tooting her horn as she swept past.

Her bodyguard's car pulled away from the kerb and followed her. She only hoped the man didn't know about the rear driveway at Chris's place. But if he did, why should he think it significant? She'd seen him eyeing her sports car and the lavish interior of Jamieson House. His priority was to prevent someone gatecrashing her beautiful life. Never in a million years would he suppose she was planning to escape from it. And that was why it worked. At Chris's house, Stacey waved the guard to park his car in the street. While he settled down to wait patiently for her, she simply drove along the side of the house, out into the back lane and was gone, swallowed up in the network of Sydney's streets.

She almost got away with it.

It was Hal who tracked her down. He found her at two in the morning in a motel outside Taree. He didn't even knock. Stacey, tossing sleeplessly on one of the awful beds, heard the lock click once and shot upright. Another click and she was at the door, heart pounding like a big bass drum, her ear pressed against the painted woodwork. She fell on the floor when the door opened on to her—and stayed there, looking up at Hal. The sight of him warmed her, even as the grim set of his mouth told her why he was here.

'You've come to take me back.'

'Your father thought you might have come to me,' he said, closing the door behind him, pocketing the bunch of odd-looking keys. 'Apparently our tryst in the conservatory has planted the suspicion in his mind that I have some fatal attraction for you, or that I'm out to feather my nest with your fortune. I was very nearly hanged on the nearest gum tree! Naturally, when I convinced him that his little girl was not with me, he insisted that I find you. He seems to think I'd have more chance than someone else.'

'He was right, wasn't he?' Stacey said bitterly. 'How did you know I was taking this direction?'

'Your friends at Coe's told me—oh, not directly. We talked, and it came up that you'd been asking questions about the Pacific Highway route. I've visited every motel and hotel along this stretch looking for a laden Alfa sports.' He held out his hand and she took it, and was hauled to her feet. It brought her close to him. Neither of them moved.

'Dad insisted you look for me? You didn't have to do it.'

'He doesn't consider my debt repaid,' said Hal with a bitterness that matched her own. 'And nor do I.'

She stared at him. If only it wasn't Hal! If it was one of those other beefy men, she could handle them. They were only doing it for money. But Hal—Hal had his own reasons for doing things, and Hal wouldn't be handled. But still, this was the twentieth century, for heaven's sake. She was twenty-one years old. Her father had no jurisdiction over her. He couldn't have her dragged back kicking and screaming—it was Gothic.

'He means to have you back,' Hal said softly, as if he guessed her thoughts. Tiredly he stripped off his jacket and tossed it on a chair. Somewhere she had a film yet to be developed of him wearing that jacket, rolling up his sea-splashed trousers, glowering his reluctance to be photographed. He filled the tiny electric jug and dropped teabags into two thick motel cups. While the jug boiled, vibrating the crockery and spoons on the flimsy counter, he set his hands on his hips and looked around at the cheap interior, the worn, flattened carpet, the single and double beds, both disturbed.

'Perhaps home is the place you ought to be,' he said. 'You certainly don't belong in a dump like this.' He went over and tested the beds. 'Tried them both and found them lacking, Goldilocks?' he mocked. 'They're not bad, as budget beds go. You might have had to manage with worse. Not what you're used to.'

'Maybe I'm not travelling alone. Have you thought of that?' snapped Stacey, aping his hands-on-hips stance. 'Maybe there's a man in the bathroom who'll come and throw you out——'

Hal laughed shortly. 'There's no man.' His eyes flicked over her tossed hair, bare legs, the thin nightgown. 'If you had a man with you, Stacey, only one bed would be disturbed.'

The jug bubbled over. Hal switched it off and made the tea. The scars on his hand were uncovered now, red and ugly, some barbed with the marks of stitches. Handing her a cup, he sat down on the edge of the single bed. 'In your note, you said you were going to make a new life for yourself. Your father said you have only a few hundred dollars in cash and no access to your inheritance for as long as he wants it that way. How did you plan on living?'

'I have things I can sell,' she told him defiantly, refusing to speak of her getaway in the past tense. Yet.

'Like what?'

'Jewellery. The car.'

'None of it would fetch what you imagine. When you desperately need money, buyers know. It wouldn't be one of those nice, civilised deals your mother makes with antique jewellers. You've never had to sell something because you *had* to—you'd be a gift to some smart dealer. The rich girl on her uppers, unused to wheeling and dealing for survival.'

'They wouldn't know I was rich,' Stacey pointed out.

'Honey, it's written all over you.' He looked around, then went on flatly, 'If you were prepared to live like this, of course, you might get enough to pay a few months' rent and buy a cheap car. If you wanted something classier, your money would run out fast. How did you propose to eat?'

'Eat?' She found a denim jacket and pulled it around her shoulders. Among the clothes she'd smuggled out there was no dressing-gown, no *peignoir,* few of the beautiful fripperies she loved.

'You know. Meals—food. What about your other expenses? A cheaper car would break down. No Alex to obligingly fix it for you. Have you any idea how much it costs just to have a car serviced?' Hal paused a moment and went on, suddenly angry. She wondered why he was so angry. 'Of course you haven't got a clue!' he accused as if it was a mortal sin. He thrust out his hand, spread his fingers and ticked them off one by one. 'What about petrol costs, car registration, third party insurance, rent, clothes, medical expenses? All the things you never had to think about because they're taken care of—all the things Daddy gives you an allowance for or that you put on credit. How would you live without Daddy's allowance and your little bits of plastic, Stacey, tell me that?'

'I'd work, of course,' she said, thrusting out her chin. 'I'm a photographer, remember?'

Hal gave a derisive snort. 'You mean, taking pictures? You think there's a living to be made in that dilettante girl photographer stuff you do? Indulging yourself in nature shots and slumming it to steal the dignity of some poor bloody derelict just because it makes a nice composition? You call that work—doggie portraits for self-indulgent divorcees who spend more money on their dogs than some people get to spend on their children? That's a hobby you've got, kid. You'd starve if ever you had to earn your living at it.'

'Don't be such a snob! Rich divorcees, believe it or not, get just as lonely as poor divorcees. The difference is they have money to spend on consolation . . . and I wouldn't starve. *Won't* starve. I'll survive, don't you doubt it for a minute!' She stabbed a finger at his chest.

'And where were you planning to launch this instantly brilliant, successful career of yours?' he goaded. 'Among your rich friends under Daddy's nose?'

'No!' she snapped. 'Where I'm not known. This isn't just a jaunt to cover my tracks. I'm on my way to Bris—on my way north. I'm not stupid.'

A pause. His anger eased. 'Not stupid, no—ignorant. A babe in the woods. You wouldn't last five minutes without someone to show you the way.' He took his teacup over to the counter, let it clatter down, then looked steadily at her. 'It's a good thing I found you. You're a hothouse plant, Stacey, and you saw what happened to the hothouse plants when they were exposed to the rough side of life. Better go back where you belong.'

'Where I belong? Pardon me, but haven't you been trying to tell me I should make a change?'

'You've left it too late.'

It tore at her confidence. After her initial emotion at leaving she had been excited, viewing the future as an adventure begun with hoodwinking her guard. This shabby, cheap room had removed any element of adventure, woken her to the realities. Even before Hal had come she was questioning her own ability to function without the support structure of the life she had known. His harsh résumé of the facts echoed doubts that had already risen to taunt her. Maybe she *was* too accustomed to luxury. Maybe she *didn't* have the strength to survive without help. Perhaps she would be a washout as a photographer and wouldn't be able to earn a living. She turned away from him. Damned if she would let him see how scared she was! That pathetic little man had scared her with his threats, but this was worse in a way. Not one man lurking to shoot her down, but life itself.

'It's two-thirty. Get some sleep. We'll leave in the morning,' said Hal.

The flat authority of it bolstered Stacey. She whirled on him, eyes blazing. Anger was a welcome, positive thing that silenced the voices of self-doubt. Imitating his former tone, she drawled, 'And how were you planning to get me out of here? Gag me? Tie me up? Slip me a—a Mickey Finn or hold me at gunpoint?'

'Don't be stupid, Stacey!'

'I don't intend to make it easy for you. I'll yell—I'll scream——' Her eyes gleamed as she backed away from him. 'In fact, if I screamed right now that could just take care of you . . . you used housebreaking tools to get in here. That's illegal . . .' Stacey slipped off her denim jacket, held it dramatically for a moment between thumb and finger, then dropped it to the floor. She hooked her foot under the tiny, flimsy coffee-table. It flipped over and the regulation glass ashtray did a double bounce and bumped into the wall. ' "Oh, officer, I was asleep and this horrible brute forced his way in here and started to—to——" ' She inserted a finger beneath the delicate shoestring strap of her nightie and tugged at it. There was a sharp, tearing sound. ' "Oh, it was *too* awful—he just grabbed me and I struggled——" ' She sidled up to the double bed and tossed the pillows on the floor, swiped her purse and car keys from the bedside table. They fell with a clatter on the thin carpet. ' "I *kicked* him, and he swore and cursed and—and tore my nightdress——" ' She took the nightgown hem in both hands. The fabric rent with a silken hiss, and Stacey caught at her bodice just in time as the strapless side flopped down. She put a catch in her voice. ' "He was so big and strong, and he pushed me down on the bed and I—I just screamed——" '

Stacey's mouth opened wide, but Hal launched himself

through space and knocked her backwards on to the double bed, his hand planted over her lower face. Furiously she squirmed and pushed and tried to get her knee up, but the tired bounce of the bed absorbed the shock of her most aggressive blows and sucked her down into its worn intimacy. She stopped after a few moments. The terrible bed could not distinguish between emotions. Her anger was the force that moved it, but it rocked and creaked in a suggestive, time-worn rhythm. Hal's weight pressed down on top of her, her legs sprawled, her hips thrust up against him with every lewd jounce of the cheap springs. Her struggles stopped, and her mouth moved impotently beneath his hand. She glared at him over it.

'Why does that look familiar?' he murmured. His breath touched warmly at her temple. The bed gave up reluctantly, its sensual surges slowly lessening, its voice dying from excited, high-pitched groans to sighs. And silence.

'I could have already slipped you a Mickey Finn in your tea,' he said, amused. Her eyes widened, and she made some muffled sounds against his palm. Hal gave a low laugh and the bed trembled. 'No, I didn't, but I'm beginning to wish I had.' He picked up the loose night-gown strap. Threads hung from the torn end. 'My God, you would have done it too, wouldn't you? Screamed, accused me of assault with intent to rape, and made your escape while I sorted out my reputation. You're quite a girl!' He removed his hand from her mouth.

'Don't patronise me!' Stacey lashed out at him. It was a mistake. The bed heaved. 'I've had all that from you—all the "you could be quite a woman" stuff. You hypocrite! You were the one who told me if I ever wanted the things that mattered I'd have to face up to the nasties and things that go bump in the night! And if I don't try now, I'm scared——' To her chagrin, her throat closed over.

Swallowing, she went on angrily,' Scared that if I don't make a break now I'll just—give in. I'm all they have, and they want me safe. They want me to live the life they've planned for me—a life they genuinely believe is best for me, and I love them. Don't you understand how easy it would be for me to go along with it? Not everyone has *your* strength—I'm not so stupid as to think I could change my life if I stayed. You don't understand what a powerful structure my family is. I could fight against it for a while, but it's too strong. And part of me *wants* to stay and enjoy all the good things, part of me *wants* to please them——' She jerked free of him, sat up on the bed and pushed back her hair. 'If I want to change things, I have to get away to reduce the odds. If I go back, it has to be with the strength already built in to resist—don't you see what I mean?' Almost panting for breath, she stopped. Hal was propped up on one elbow, apparently unmoved by her plea. For it *was* a plea, Stacey realised, hating herself for stooping to it. 'No, of course you don't,' she said stormily. 'You don't *want* to see my viewpoint. You have to believe that this is just another little whim of the spoiled heiress, another thoughtless jaunt. Well, it wasn't easy walking out like that, letting everyone think I'd be back later as usual. It was awful, awful! I couldn't even kiss my mother good-bye——' She dashed the easy tears from her eyes. 'You'd prefer to think this is some mindless, attention-getting exercise. You want to convince yourself that I wouldn't have a chance in hell of succeeding, because that way you can take me back without any twinges of conscience.'

'You don't know what you're talking about.' Hal swung his legs off the bed and Stacey lunged to grab his arm.

'Babysitting a spoiled heiress, even saving her from plastic surgery, would never have evened the score, would it, Hal? But taking me back! Recapturing the runaway!

Now *that* would wipe out your debt to my father, wouldn't it?'

Stonily he looked at her, his face an enigmatic mask in the lamplight. 'Get some sleep.'

Again she held him back, grabbing his arm, digging her fingers in. 'I'm right, aren't I? Your precious pride can't let you be beholden. I suppose your family is crushed under the terrible burden of owing somebody a favour—but never fear, hero Hal is galloping to the rescue, hauling home the heiress to balance the account!' Frustration and rage boiled over and she took a childish swipe at him, tears spilling over, her voice thickening. 'Well, I hope it'll make you feel better when your stiff-necked pride is restored. Will you have a celebration?'

'Stacey——' Hal dodged her flying fists, got a hold on her arms and pinned them to her sides. Her sobs became noisy gulps. Tears rushed unchecked down her face. 'Stacey, sweetheart——' he muttered, and pulled her close, cradling her head against his shoulder while she cried out the strain of the one-sided goodbyes, the disillusionment of reality, the disappointment of discovery. After a while, she pushed him away. 'I hate you,' she said. There was no heat in it. He half smiled.

'I hope it makes you feel better.'

They stared at each other. The small, shabby room seemed to shrink. Hal's eyes skated away from hers, downwards. He reached over and took the dangling night-gown strap between finger and thumb again, twitched it upwards. Stacey looked to see the sheer fabric slide up to cover the upper slope of her breast. She'd forgotten about that, she hadn't felt the exposure. It would have been natural to raise her hands and push his away, make the adjustment herself, but she didn't.

'You need a pin.' Hal held the strap taut against her shoulder. Her eyes rose slowly to his.

'Yes,' she whispered, conscious of the warmth of his hand against her skin. She felt his fine tremor, saw his stillness as he held on to a breath, then expelled it in a rush of warm air that laced across her chest. The strap wavered, lowered. Hal reversed his movement, tugged gently on it until the fine pink silk of her nightgown bodice peeled away with it. His fingertips lightly sketched the contours of her exposed breast, delicately explored the lower fullness, ghosted over the pale tan areola that crinkled in response. With that same light touch he slipped the other strap down to loop over her arm, so that her breasts were both bared. Stacey sighed, leaned back a little, supporting herself and not touching him, just watching him caress her. He lowered her on to the bed and she held him to her breast, gasping her delight as his lips caressed and sipped and sucked. And all the while his hands moved on her, drawing down the nightgown so that she was naked to his touch. Stacey pulled his shirt buttons free, scissoring her fingers to catch and tug at his dark chest hair. How many times she had longed to touch him like this. He was rough and smooth.

'Hal——' she sighed, breathing in his scent, that familiar blend of all things Hal. Urgently she held him as he stroked her, roused her. Her hands swept from his broad, beautiful back to slide over his taut behind. She lay welcoming beneath him, and stilled in the moment he did. Her body clamoured for fulfilment, but she knew there would be none. There was no logic to it, just some intuitive feeling that now was not the right time. Not yet—maybe never. But, however depressing that prospect, it made no difference. They might never be together again like this, but it wasn't a good enough reason to make love.

Stacey closed her eyes and held him and tried to think why it would not be right on this night. No reason offered itself, but the conviction remained. That didn't stop the waves of regret, nor the physical pangs of frustration. Nor the mental bargaining: You've gone this far, isn't it coy to stop now? You mightn't see him again and you're half in love with the man—take what you can—come on! Nor did it stop her mind running away beyond this frozen pose of passion. She imagined stripping away the rest of his clothes, imagined his confined hardness released, imagined taking him inside her and the bed beginning its ride—slowly this time, long, slow, languid waves gathering speed, gathering depth—faster—faster. Stacey didn't move a muscle. Perspiration gathered on her forehead. Hal raised his head and looked down at her. There was perspiration on his brow, too. His eyes were dilated. She giggled, not sure whether she wanted to laugh or cry.

'Is this what you meant by "things that go bump in the night"?'

It was a release of tension. Laughing, they rolled apart and retrieved their clothes. Laughing, they dressed. But then their laughter died. Everything had its duality. Nothing was ever entirely happy or entirely sad.

'Get some sleep,' said Hal. He reached out briefly and touched her hand.

She wouldn't sleep. But if he did, she would quietly gather up her things and be gone before he woke. If he slept.

He did. She waited an hour to be sure. Hal was still, his breathing deep and regular. Stacey found a spare blanket and pillow in the wardrobe, arranged them in the bed in a bolster shape. Critically, she thought it just might pass muster in the dark. Packing her things was a nightmare. She tiptoed around, heart in her mouth, stifling a cry when she hit her shin on something. Carefully, monitoring Hal's sleeping form, she opened the slats of the awful venetian blind just enough to let in some moonlight so that she wouldn't crash into something and wake him. With the light she was quicker; she collected her few toiletries and slid them into her bag, then, with another glance at Hal, she stripped off her nightgown. Naked, she groped for clean underwear in her bag, her hands trembling in her haste. Several times she tossed an anxious glance at him, but he didn't move. Just as well, she thought, suppressing a slightly hysterical giggle. She didn't want him waking up to witness another strip-tease!

Quick. Panties, yes—forget about a bra. Urgency made her clumsy. Adrenalin was flooding her system, making her heart pound, her mouth dry. She stepped into the brief red panties and pulled on her jeans. She'd never realised how loud denim was. She inched the jeans on bit by bit, wiggling her hips into them, her breasts jiggling madly. Biting her lip, she eased up the zipper. It sounded like a muffled motorbike. Hal stirred and pulled at the bedclothes, raising an arm across his face. Stacey froze, and stayed that way for what seemed an age, just to be sure. The air was cold on her bare breasts, but she shivered silently as Hal gave a sigh and shuffled again. At last it seemed safe, and cautiously she put on her sweater. Mohair was quiet, at any rate; she must make a note of that for future reference—if at any time in her rather hazy future she might have to dress like a fugitive again. Denim was noisy, mohair was quiet. Stacey held down another giggle. Nerves were making her a little high.

Ready, she looked reflectively at Hal, then tiptoed to his jacket which hung on the awful armchair. Not very hopefully she felt in the pockets, wincing at the sharp clink of metal. His car keys! Careless of you, Hal, very careless, she thought gleefully, picturing his face when he woke. When he woke . . . She studied him. The bedclothes had sheared sideways, and the pale moonlight slatted across a broad, bare expanse of back and shoulder. All that rustling in the dark must have been him taking off his clothes. He was probably sleeping in his pants. The idea was immensely interesting, but she wouldn't let herself dwell on it. Instead she crept around until she found his discarded shirt and trousers. A few furtive pats revealed a soft wallet in the pocket. Gingerly she went through it. There was cash and several credit cards, his driver's licence. Biting her lip, she looked at him. Oh, Stacey, that would be mean! But her shoulders moved silently in laughter. No clothes, no car keys, no money, no identification and no explanation as to why he was in a motel where he hadn't even registered! Oh, Hal! It was too much —she almost broke up, reached out to leave the wallet, then changed her mind, her amusement suddenly giving way to pragmatism. She might as well give herself as long a start as possible. And Hal was a big boy; he could look after himself.

With his clothes slung over her arm, his wallet carefully pushed down into her bag, Stacey paused, frowning. Hal might remain obligated to her father without the grand gesture of returning the lamb to the fold, and she was sorry about that. She couldn't understand why he felt that way, but she undertood that it was important to him. But she couldn't let him take her back just so that he could clear his feelings of obligation. Hal would have to find some other way to wipe out the debt he thought he owed.

Nevertheless, she tiptoed over and looked down at his sleeping face, moved by longing and deep regret. 'Goodbye, Hal,' she whispered, stopping herself just short of kissing his scarred hand. She lingered a last few moments, almost hoping to be discovered before she could commit herself and maybe fail. But he didn't wake. Quietly, she left.

CHAPTER SEVEN

THE MONTH of March was officially autumn, and summer was over, but in Brisbane not many noticed. Summer suntans deepened, boats bobbed lazily on Moreton Bay or were moored at the remote and beautiful beaches of its islands, the south coast hosted its weekend crowds and suburban Brisbane basked and bathed and barbecued. The nights were milder, more comfortable after the high humidity and evening storms of a sub-tropical summer that had sent the plant life into a frenzy of growth. Banana trees and avocados, palms, frangipani and the glorious orchid-tree, poinciana and umbrella trees, rampant cerise bougainvillaea and yellow-trumpeted allamanda. Always some variety of jasmine bloomed, its scent a permanent, scarcely noticed underscoring in older suburbs like this one. Always on weekends, the smell of cut grass and jasmine, and somewhere the tantalising, smoky odour of barbecuing meat and onions. Here, near the river, weekdays or weekends—always mosquitoes.

'Gotcha!' Stacey slapped a mosquito off her arm and handed the barbecue fork to Paul. 'Your turn. I'm being eaten alive out here!'

Paul hooked an arm about her waist, giving a Dracula leer even as he expertly flipped sizzling chops and burgers. 'I've come to help the mosquitoes, my dear.' He nuzzled a kiss into her neck, but Stacey disengaged before it could develop. He left his arm curved there in mid-air, empty, and looked mock-seriously at it. 'One minute you have her, the next you don't!'

120

She laughed. 'The one that got away, Paul? Am I spoiling your record?'

Paul pulled a face. 'I suppose my sister has been telling you untruths about me again—don't trust her. You must be more careful about who you share with in future. Now me, for instance——' He caught her hand and placed it over his heart '—I'd be such a nice flatmate.'

'Why?' she challenged.

'Well—I've got such a nice flat, for a start.'

'I like it where I am,' Stacey smiled, inclining her head towards the old house she shared with serious Scottish Liz, Graham and Paul's sister Jenny. She hadn't liked it so much at first, but then, she hadn't been accustomed to sharing. She'd moved three times since coming to Brisbane over eighteen months ago—from a grotty hostel to a less grotty single flat to this, each move coinciding with a better paid job. This house was old and cheap, but it had character and its garden was a tropical tangle of palms and passionfruit vines, and there was the river at their back door and an ancient skiff in which to paddle on long, warm evenings. Tonight there were coloured lights strung with the same abandon as the passionfruit vines, between the house on its tall, gangling timber stumps and the clumped golden cane palms. Chairs and tables lurched on the uneven lawn. A loudspeaker, roped to the latticework of the house's undercroft, crackled, then started up with Dire Straits; close around it, people danced.

'Not Dire Straits again!' exclaimed Stacey. 'That's three times in a row! I'll go and find something else before we all go crazy to "Walk of Life".'

'Runaway Stacey,' Paul said sorrowfully. 'I wish you'd look over your shoulder at me.'

She stopped and did just that. 'Look over my shoulder?'

'You're always looking over your shoulder, physically

and metaphorically. I can never decide if you're frightened of something, or hoping something—or someone—will catch you.'

Stacey gave him a companionable slap on the rear. 'This is a party, Paul—don't start spouting your third-year psychology! We'll all end up depressed.'

'Or *manic!*' He bared his teeth, rolled his eyes and deftly flipped a wayward sausage back on to the hotplate. Stacey went away laughing but impressed. Paul might appear casual about his studies and act the fool at parties, but he was keenly observant. Runaway Stacey. She'd had to keep her eyes open, look over her shoulder, lest her father's people find her. Lest Hal find her. If anyone did, it would be him, she'd reasoned. Which made Paul's observations all the more interesting. On the one hand she had been afraid that Hal, representing her father, might turn up and put an end to her freedom. But on the other . . . She slapped another mosquito into oblivion and waved down a chorus of protests which turned to approval as she turned off the music and put on a John Farnham tape. Then she lifted a tray of drinks, waiter-style, on the backturned flat of her hand. One of her survival skills, she thought.

Liz caught her arm and whispered urgently, 'What's with Jenny and Graham?' She pointed to their flatmates who were dancing in a mild sort of clinch. 'The four of us promised it was all to be kept platonic!' She said 'platonic' as only a Scot could, with a juicy 'L' sound and an accusatory lilt at the end. She went on in the same tone, 'Have you got the coleslaw?'

'What are you going to do with it?' Stacey laughed. 'Toss it over them instead of a bucket of cold water?'

'If I thought it would work, I would,' Liz said gloomily. 'It will really mess things up if those two come to the boil.'

Stacey couldn't agree more. She'd had her suspicions for a while that Jenny and Graham were straying from the platonic, but there wasn't much they could do about it. She told Liz where to find the coleslaw, handed around the drinks and ran up the back steps to fetch a camera for some candids.

The walls of her bedroom were covered with candids. In those first dismal months on her own she'd taken photo graphs the way a child clung on to a scrappy bit of baby blanket. Films and processing had eaten into her precious cash reserve, but she needed to do it. It made her feel less of a speck in her new world, to capture it on film. Nowadays it amused her to see the prints in chronological order. A view of the hostel where she'd stayed for two months—in black and white, a ground-level view, and very appropriate too. Then there was a sort of kitchen still-life taken in the snack bar where she'd had her first waitressing job—a dented saucepan, empty caterer's size sauce bottle and the cook's cigarette, half ash and still wisping smoke. A crumpled paper place mat with the motif 'Sid's Snacks'. Sid had thought she was a spy from the Health Department, and only a free portrait of his family had convinced him otherwise. There was the sombre post-war block of flats at Milton where Stacey had lived alone, and lonelier even than in the hostel. She'd shot it with black and white infra-red film at a slow speed with a blurred jogger running past, which had seemed a nice, ironic touch to one who had to live there. A severe architectural study of the employment office with its lovely landscaped garden and its waiting, aimless people on their weekly outing, smoking cigarettes on a bench out front. The mock Tudor pub where she'd learned the hard way how to carry six glasses of beer, two vodkas and a brandy on a slippery tray; the bookshop where she'd worked, shops and faces from the shopping centre where she'd shouted bargains over a microphone. Self-portraits along the way—Stacey Jamieson in metamorphosis. Faces of friends made in unexpected places, unknown faces in the crowd, her visions of the river and the city and its wonderful flowering trees, and finally a picture of herself taking a picture of herself, reflected in the bronze window of Marshall Studios where she'd finally landed a job in photography.

'Stacey James, this is your life,' Liz had said when she'd seen the montage of photographs. 'Or a wee bit of it, anyway.'

Right the first time, Stacey had thought. It might only be a 'wee bit' of it, but it *was* her life, the only part of it she knew she had really lived herself, even if it was with another name. Lived and laughed and cried and cursed. She wouldn't forget the rain in this part of her life.

Stacey aimed the flash at the wall full of pictures to test it, and the white light bounced back, momentarily blinding her. She was almost to the back stairs when the doorbell rang. It was just auible over the stereo throb of Farnham singing 'No One Comes Close'.

'Oh, darn it!' she muttered, grimacing. None of their guests went through the formality of front doors, but simply strolled around to the back garden. This must be Mrs Bartlett from across the road, complaining about the noise. Stacey rehearsed a couple of soothing, apologetic phrases on her way to the door. Maybe she should offer to photograph Mrs Bartlett's cat as a palliative for their parties. She opened the door, wearing her best neighbourly smile. 'Mrs Bartlett, I'm very sorry if we're making too much——' She peered into the shadows at the rather un-Bartlett-like shape waiting there. Whoever it was remained very still—very still. It was the quality of the stillness that told her who it was. No one could stand as still as him when he wanted. '—noise,' she croaked. The booming bass was in her ears, all around her. For a year and a half she had been expecting, fearing and contrarily hoping for this, but self-preservation had become such a priority that within seconds of recognising him, Stacey threw up the camera and squeezed the button so that the flash-gun released, blinding blue-white. She had a tantalising glimpse of Hal's face, then she spun around, slammed the door and prepared to run.

It all went wrong, of course. He got his shoulder wedged in and she kept trying to shut the door, when any fool could have seen that no door would shut with Hal Stevens' shoulder stuck in it. And where would she run to anyway, supposing she shut him out? There was the back door, but he knew where she lived now, so what was the point? But she couldn't stop resisting him. The reflex was too ingrained after keeping it sharpened for such a long time.

'So you've found me!' she panted, pitting her weight against him. Another few months, that was all she needed. She would have written to her parents this time instead of a furtive phone call too short to be traced, and given them her address. 'Big deal! But it doesn't matter much now. I was going to tell them where I was any day——' Damn, damn! She had so wanted to reappear when *she* decided to, on her own terms, not to be tracked down, found out, reported on. It was a matter of pride. 'Oh, *damn* you, Hal!'

'Stacey, there's a very interested lady watching us from across the road. If you don't want the police around, you'd better let me in.'

She fell back, clutching her Hasselblad, and Hal walked in, then closed the door. Hal. Her heart gave another jolt that had nothing to do with flight or fear of discovery. For a long time they just looked at each other, curiously checking out the familiar things against memory, seeking the changes. His face looked a fraction thinner, the bold bone-structure sharpened, the clefts and hollows of his face more deeply shadowed. He was deeply tanned and his hair was longer, wavy, sun-bleached from dark brown to dark gold. The hands-on-hips pose dragged his T-shirt across his shoulders and chest, accentuating the pure, beautiful male lines of his body. Stacey's eyes slid slowly in self-indulgence down the bulge of his bicep, elbow, hair-spattered forearm to his right hand. The scars were white now, standing out against his tan like random chalk marks She remembered the glass splinters trembling where those marks were, remembered the superb control that had over-ridden the natural withdrawal from pain that would have allowed those splinters to reach her face. Stacey directed a swift glance at Hal's left hand, and felt a surge of relief when she saw there was no wedding band. Don't be silly—doesn't mean a thing, she thought. Lots of married men don't wear them. But don't ask, not again.

Hal walked over to her, and for a moment she thought he was trying to get a look at *her* left hand, which was curved about the camera. But he touched the flash-gun and smiled.

'The fastest gun in the West? Is it something new in self-defence—"Stop or I'll do a portrait of you"?'

She laughed shakily. 'In other circumstances it might have given me an edge. How did you find me, Hal?'

He paced away a little, looking at the living-room cluttered with old reclaimed sofas and rugs, Graham's piles of magazines, Jenny's piano, Liz's spinning wheel and fat hanks of hand-dyed wool, her own sepia portrait of Liz and Jenny fitted into an old oval frame to match the age of the house. He leaned out of the window to look at the barbecue going on below. 'With great difficulty,' he said. 'Going to offer me a hamburger, Stacey? I'm starved!'

'Invite the spy to dinner—why should I? You *are* here

to spy on me, aren't you? I suppose you'll phone my father and tell him my address and give him a run-down on my friends!'

Hal leaned a shoulder against the wall in the pose she recalled so well. Brown eyes held hers steadily. 'You said you were going to do it yourself soon. Does that mean you've achieved what you set out to achieve?'

'I haven't set the world on fire,' she said ruefully. 'I really thought I would at first, you know. The confidence of ignorance. But the hothouse plant survived, Hal.' Eyes gleaming at the long-awaited chance to make him eat his words, she tapped him on the chest. 'All your dire predictions were wrong. I didn't run home to Daddy, and I managed without allowances and credit cards—I survived. Admit you were wrong.'

'I must be. You opened the door apologising as if you were used to it. I remember when it was a brass band occasion for Stacey Jamicson to say "I'm sorry".' Ah yes—she remembered the day she'd apologised to him in her car. In the rain. 'And,' he went on, 'I've been here all of ten minutes and you haven't asked yet if I'm married.'

Stacey refused the trap, pressed her lips tight together. Hal chuckled. 'I'm not,' he said.

Liz came in just then. 'Now it's hamburgers and holding hands! I just hope they don't get lovey over breakfast. I don't think I could take that with my corn-flakes—oh!' She hugged the empty coleslaw bowl and stared at Hal. 'Hello. I don't think we've met.'

'Liz, this is Hal,' Stacey said baldly.

The Scottish girl studied him carefully, especially the dimension of his shoulders and chest, his underarm-to-waist measurement. 'This is never the Sweater Man?' she exclaimed.

'No, no. Stevens—Hal Stevens,' Stacey said hastily.

'He's staying for the barbecue.' Liz went to the kitchen to refill the coleslaw bowl, and Stacey led Hal outside. Before she introduced him around she said, 'They don't know about my background.'

'So I gathered, Stacey James,' he said drily. 'It was an obvious alias. I thought you'd pick it. I had an old friend check the photographic studios for a Stacey Jamieson or James.'

'How did you know I was in Brisbane?'

'You gave it away in the motel that night.'

'How did you know I wouldn't change my first name?' she asked.

'I just knew.'

'Huh! So I'm an open book to you?'

Hal's smile was faint, his eyes intent. 'You telegraph a few moves now and then.'

Stacey pulled a face. So that was how he'd found her. With intuition and a slip of the tongue she thought she'd covered and the help of a friend. Some friend! Quite a job, running through the photo studios from A to M. She eyed Hal with even more interest, if it was possible. It wasn't only rich men who could call in favours. But Hal would do it in an entirely different way. She knew a sudden sadness that her father hadn't been able to find her. It probably hadn't occurred to him that her photography might be her means of support. He never had taken it or her ambitions very seriously. Very likely he had directed few or no enquiries to studios.

Hal had found her because he was in tune with her in some way, because he'd listened to her. Perhaps because he had called on a friend for help, rather than on hired assistance. Ah, Dad, she thought, why couldn't you have been in tune with me and listened and therefore known what I might be seeking, where I might go? But then there might have been no need to run. She bit her lip.

'It's a sprawling city,' Hal said softly. 'And you could have settled anywhere between the Gold Coast and Cairns.'

Stacey's eyes flicked up to him. She *was* an open book, wasn't she? 'You found me,' she said.

'Yes.' He let the single word stand alone for maybe twenty seconds, then took her arm. 'Introduce me to your new friends, Stacey James. I won't blow the whistle on you.'

'Not yet, anyway,' she said with a darkling look.

'Not yet,' he agreed, looking amused and, yes, smug. 'Will you introduce me as an old boyfriend?'

'Why not my old hairdresser?' she said, a malicious sparkle in her eyes. Hal set a hand on his hip.

'Ooh!' he said, and she threw back her head and laughed.

It was a peculiar feeling to have Hal here in her new life, mixing with her new friends. One part of her liked it, one part tingled with pleasure every time she turned around and glimpsed his rugged face highlighted blue or red or yellow by the coloured lights. But one part resented it—the part that wasn't quite ready to let the past back in. Hal had pre-empted her attempts to handle it her own way, do it in her own time. She chewed her lip, consulted her watch and wondered if she should get in before him after all, and phone her parents with her address. Prompted by Hal catching up with her, it would not be the firm declaration of independence that she'd so wanted, but it was better than the alternative. 'I've found your daughter for you, Brian' would smack of lost property being located.

Hal was laughing with Liz, who had managed to insert herself betwen Jenny and Graham. Did Hal still feel obligated to her father, then, that he should look for her so long afterwards? Stacey was impatient with the idea. After all, he had put in a month of his time protecting her, a month away from his own business interests, which must have been costly and inconvenient, and he had saved her from disfigurement. Surely he could feel his debt repaid, regardless of what her father might have said at the shock of her running away? It was silly male pride and stiff-necked notions of honour unsatisfied. If Hal wanted to cling to such outdated feelings, it was none of her business.

Nevertheless, half-way up the steps she hesitated. If she beat Hal to it and phoned her father, the silly fool would lose his last chance to balance the ledger, according to his way of thinking. She had robbed him of that chance when she'd escaped him at the motel, but there had been more at stake then. Now that she'd been standing on her own two feet for so long, perhaps she was strong enough to stand the pressure without her grand gesture. Which meant that this time she could let Hal make his. She owed him something. From here she could see the scars on his hand, but she ran a hand over her face and imagined them there instead. Not that they would have remained there long. Her father would have had her whisked off to a plastic surgeon wherever in the world he could find the best, and she would have been caught up for months and months in treatment and maybe never again found the courage to break away. Still . . . she took a step up towards the house, wistfully running through the 'prodigal daughter' phrases she had been composing for months. And mentally abandoning them.

Before she could turn to descend again, Hal caught her arm from behind. 'They're probably not at home,' he said, infuriatingly tuned in to her. Stacey glared at him as he drew her down the steps.

'I'm surprised you can spare the time to come haring after me. Haven't you got your hands full with the martial arts academy and Cedar Hill?' She had seen an advert for Cedar Hill in the newspaper a few months back. It had given her pleasure to think of Hal realising his dream. It had also given her a few flutters of apprehension when she'd looked up the location on a map and discovered Cedar Hill was over the border and only about two hours' drive from Brisbane.

'I sold out my share of the school,' Hal told her with a twist of his lips. 'Nowadays I'm at the farm full-time. Come and dance with me.'

Her eyes gleamed. She had asked him to dance at her party. Astonishing to discover how much his refusal still rankled. 'A dance with your ex-client, the rich young thing?' she mocked. 'A bit of a novelty?'

'I want to talk to you.'

'I have guests,' she smiled. 'Goodness, but this conversation gives me a feeling of *déjà vu*——' He gripped her wrist, gave the merest tug that jerked her off the steps and into his arms. In one continuous movement he danced her away to the pool of shadow beneath a poinciana, where the music was less intrusive.

'Brute force! Now, why didn't I think of that?' Stacey said lightly, and aimed a blow at his upper arm. Hal grunted in surprise. 'Mosquito,' she explained, smiling sweetly. 'The penalty for living on the river.'

He chuckled at that. They danced, and Hal wanted to know what she'd done and where she'd worked, and she told him with a certain pride, leaving out the self-pity and the sharp pain of separation from all that was familiar. As usual, he seemed to read between the lines.

'It's hard leaving home,' he told her. 'I was nineteen when I took off, and I couldn't wait to be out from under parental rule and nagging. You know what I missed? Dad complaining about where I'd parked my car and Mum nagging me to take Vitamin C. I gave up vitamin C on principle when I left home,' he smiled. 'Came down with a terrible dose of 'flu!'

She smiled too, but for all his easy words she felt the tension in him. He was almost as tense as she was. Perhaps there was a late storm brewing, one of those sudden tropical bursts preceded by humidity and the zap of excess electricity in the air.

'I'm here because of Grace,' he told her, and she gaped at him.

'Grace? Our Grace? Amazing Grace?'

'She said you'd been in contact with your parents, so I suppose you know Grace and Alex have been replaced.'

'Yes, Mother told me.' Stacey frowned. After the bomb incident and her father's increased preoccupation with security, it had been inevitable, but the news had profoundly depressed Stacey and made the memory of her old home that much more remote. Without Grace kneading her bread in the kitchen and Alex working out in the House of Stoush, it would never be the same again. The end of an era. Quite fitting, really. 'Mother didn't know where they'd gone. Are they all right—how did *you* come to be talking to Grace?'

Hal moved her around to a few bars of music before he answered. 'They work for me now—at Cedar Hill. At least, Alex does; Grace is in hospital at present.'

Stacey pulled back from him, staring. Grace—lean, fit Grace who claimed her vegetarian diet made her immune to so much as a headache? 'In hospital? What's wrong—which hospital—how serious?'

He brought her close again. 'She's going to be OK. It was a cancer scare——' He tightened his arm around Stacey at her convulsive jerk. 'But they got it all. She had a hysterectomy last week and she's recovering well physically, but——'

'But? What?' urged Stacey.

'She's depressed, weepy. It's common, the doctor said, for a lot of women to go through a stage of feeling useless,

less of a woman, and apparently Grace has succumbed to it even though her childbearing days are over. But there's no logic to it, the doctor said——'

'Weepy!' echoed Stacey, alarmed at the thought of a weepy, depressed Grace. 'But she's always been so——'

'Strong, yes. Alex is doing what he can, but what would really help is if her children could visit her. It just isn't possible economically. They're scattered all around the country and can't afford the trip. You're the next closest thing she has to a daughter——'

'Where is she? Which hospital?' demanded Stacey. 'Can I see her tomorrow?'

Hal stopped dancing and looked at her in mild surprise.

'Did you think I wouldn't go?' she exclaimed.

'It's not as if it's a matter of life or death,' he shrugged. 'And you have obligations—a job.'

'Grace is special to me,' she said stiffly. 'If I can help her, then I want to. My obligations are my own business to sort out. Which hospital?'

Murwillumbah, he said, about two hours' drive south. 'One, if you still drive the way you used to,' he added tongue in cheek.

Stacey refused the bait. The music thumped on, a blatant rock rhythm too raw for the mild shuffle they were doing. It was hardly dancing, and if it was anyone else she would suggest they sit down. But it was Hal, and the feel of his arm about her waist, the warm clasp of his hand and the solidity of his shoulder beneath her hand, were all precious sensations to be gathered and stored while they might. She wondered why he hadn't simply told her about Grace when she'd first let him in, instead of joining in the barbecue, meeting a heap of strangers. She jerked back her head and stared at him.

'Is that the only reason you found me? To tell me about Grace?' He nodded. 'You—you're not still working on tracing me for Dad?' He shook his head. 'And now that you've found me—will you tell him where I am? If you still feel in his debt you could kill two birds with one stone.'

'As things have turned out, I consider my debt cancelled,' he said drily. 'I won't be hotfooting it to Brian to tell him where his little girl is.'

Stacey gave a great sigh, then stiffened. She thumped him on the chest. 'You rotter! You could have told me that instead of letting me . . . I was even thinking that I might let——' She flushed scarlet. Her serious contemplation of sacrificing her own pride for his seemed idiotic now. 'You might have said all this at the start.'

'I might,' he smiled, a peculiar gleam in his eyes. 'Has it made you suffer, brat?'

Rather warily she said, 'You know it has.'

'You don't know what suffering is.' Exerting a little extra pressure, Hal brought her back close in his arms, put his cheek against her hair. She closed her eyes and tried to channel the feeling straight into her memory bank. 'You should try waking in a motel with nothing but a pair of pants to your name!'

She giggled. 'Was it bad?'

'You could at least have left my trousers.'

'I wanted to slow you down,' she explained.

'You did,' he assured her. 'Bedsheets are hell to run in.'

Her laughter rippled out. 'Did you get your things back? I detoured two hundred kilometres to post your wallet and clothes to you.'

'I got them.'

'It was mean of me, but it was my first lesson in survival. It must have put you in a spot with Dad—me getting away like that.'

'Like you, I survived,' shrugged Hal.

'You shouldn't have fallen asleep,' she giggled. 'I was

terrified I might wake you. You've no idea how carefully I got dressed!'

His shoulders shook. 'I can imagine.'

'It *was* a rotten thing to do,' she admitted, looking in his eyes, 'but the circumstances were desperate. No hard feelings?'

'Of course not. You know what a good sport I am,' murmured Hal. He lifted a hand and brought it down in a tremendous smack on her behind. Stacey leapt with the shock of it, her eyes watered with the sting of it.

'Mosquito,' he explained, deadpan.

CHAPTER EIGHT

AT STACEY'S entrance into the hospital ward, Grace didn't even turn her head. The Olive Oyl angularity that had always seemed so dynamic, fired from within by Grace's energy, was fragile without it. Stacey wiped the concern from her face and went to the bed, dropping a kiss on Grace's cheek.

'What's a vegetarian like you doing in a place like this?' she said gently.

Grace jumped, stared at her. Tears started in her eyes and she hooked an arm around Stacey's neck, pulling her head down to her. Not so fragile, Stacey thought, her eyes watering as Grace half strangled her with affection. 'Stacey—my little Stacey! I've been that worried about you. My hat, let me look at you——' She allowed Stacey up and propped herself higher on the pillows to inspect her. 'You look so healthy!' she almost accused, as if she had no right to look healthy away from Grace's cooking. She noticed Stacey's clothes. Her voice grew stronger, she inched a bit higher on the pillows. 'Your clothes are a mess, mind.' A sniff at the creased cotton shirt and jeans. 'What's the matter—haven't you got an iron where you're living now?'

By the time Alex appeared, carrying flowers and fruit, Grace was upright, giving a piece of her mind about Stacey's abrupt departure, the decline in her dressing standards and the likelihood of her living conditions being as disappointing.

'Alex!' Stacey jumped up and hugged the man who

seemed stringier than ever. There was more grey in less hair on Alex's head now, and the leathery furrows of his face were beginning to resemble the wrinkles on his old brown boxing gloves. They're getting old, Stacey thought, surprised by the thought. Grace and Alex, growing old!

'You're a sight for sore eyes,' grinned Alex, kissing his wife and laying the gifts in her lap.

'Such a waste of money,' Grace scolded, flicking at the tissue-wrapped roses. 'A criminal waste, Alex Warman, when we've got enough expenses. The fruit I don't mind.'

Alex was delighted with this severity. He took Stacey's hand. 'She must be feeling better!'

Stacey hadn't brought fruit or flowers or books. She'd brought photographs—nothing arty, just everyday snaps taken on her automatic camera of her friends, the house where she lived, herself cleaning her battered Renault, the river. Grace bade Alex get her glasses from the drawer, and pored over the pictures, acquainting herself with Stacey's new life.

'And you share with this young fellow, you say,' she commented at a picture of Graham. 'And you so prudish you didn't like your bodyguard sleeping in the next room!'

Stacey had her questions, too. Ironically, Alex was hurt but philosophical about losing his job at Jamieson House. It was Grace who bitterly resented it, though she tried to hide it from Stacey. Hal had kept in touch with them, they told her. They had 'done' for another family for a while until Hal had Cedar Hill operating, then they moved north to work for him.

'With him, more like,' Alex amended happily.

'Do you live in one of the cabins?' asked Stacey, remembering the pepper and salt shakers that had represented ten cabins. Grace and Alex exchanged a glance.

'No, we live in the farmhouse,' Alex said.

'The original one? Hasn't Hal pulled that down yet?'

Another of those exchanged glances. Stacey felt oddly apprehensive. 'I thought the farmhouse would have to go to make way for the new buildings—the gymnasium and the dining-room.'

'Yeah, well——' Alex thumbed at his nose in his fighter's twitch. Stacey knew something was up now.

'Tell me!' she commanded. Alex waffled: things hadn't gone as fast as Hal had hoped, but he was doing all right, all things considered . . .

'He's *not* doing all right!' The words burst from Grace.

'Now, Gracie,' her husband protested, 'it's Hal's business, and he doesn't want——'

She ignored his caution. 'He's making enough to cover his mortgage repayments and wages, and that's about it. And the reason is, he couldn't get the loan he needed for building and an advertising campaign. He had to sell out his share in his karate place just to do some extensions and alterations to the farmhouse and build some showers and clear campsites, and that's all there is. And can you guess why he couldn't get an extra loan?'

Stacey blanched. No! 'Dad.' Grace nodded, her mouth tight. 'Oh, no! I knew he'd be furious, but it didn't occur to me that he might——' A few phone calls, a casual word here and there at the club. He'd used his power in Hal's favour once; this time he'd simply reversed the procedure. He could make Hal seem like a bad risk, ensure that any borrowing he did was at an impossible interest rate. Shocked and humiliated by his daughter's betrayal, he would have been looking to lay this new blame at someone's door. 'But why Hal? He came looking for me and found me, but I gave him the slip. It wasn't his fault!'

'Your father has to blame someone, and it can never be himself. He blamed Alex that night when the bomber got away, and he blamed Hal when *you* got away,' Grace told her. 'He abused him and Hal stood there and took it, but then he told Brian a few home truths about why you left—real cool and controlled, the way Hal can be, you know. And your dad—well, he was in no mood for home truths. He said he wouldn't be surprised if Hal helped you get away as he was so sympathetic, and he told Hal he'd been prepared to put in a good word for him about borrowing for the health resort, but he could forget that now. Hal said he wanted no favours, he could do it on his own, and your father said, "Well, you'd better mean that, boy, because that's just the way you'll be doing it." And he meant it.' Grace fell back against the pillows, tears in her eyes. 'I'm sorry, Stacey love. He's your father and I shouldn't have told you, but I can't forgive him for blaming my Alex the way he did and taking things out on Hal.'

For a while it seemed that Grace had taken a backward step, but when she'd wept a bit she gave a sigh, as if the outburst had given her relief.

'I'm glad you told me, Grace,' said Stacey, a determined light in her eyes. 'Now, tell me what other staff Hal has.'

No other staff. Himself and the Warmans.

'How will he manage the catering and so on while you recuperate, Grace? Can he afford to put on extra staff?'

No, he couldn't. 'But don't let on that we said that, he'll bite your head off. That's if you intend seeing Hal, of course,' Alex added slyly.

'Of course I'm going to see him, just as soon as I can organise some leave from my job . . .'

There was a handmade sign spanning the gateposts: the words 'Cedar Hill', gouged roughly out of a plank of timber. Stacey got out to open and then close the gate, for there were a few cows nosing about nearby. The track rambled through the tranquil dairy land and a dramatic stand of hoop pine, sloped steeply up and banked around to where a few cars were parked under trees. They were covered with leaves and bits of twig, as if they hadn't been used for days. Over a rise and on to a plateau to the farm house. It was a low, timber house with a red iron roof and broad verandas on three sides, with decorative timber fretwork. Tables and chairs were set out on the veranda. A big brass bell was installed by the front steps, and around it were boulders and rock plants and rosemary.

A little way from the house, in cleared sites between casuarina trees, tents were pitched, their bright yellows and tans and blues a carnival touch in a landscape of brown and green and more green. Near them was a low, rough brick block of showers and toilets, set unobtrusively among bush and boulders. From this site the ground sloped away gently at first, then in a pell-mell of boulder and windswept mountain oak and brush box, to drop majestically, vertically, into a canyon filled with piccabeen palms. The air was cool and clean—the tang of eucalyptus, the elusive smell of the bush in the morning and a lingering smokiness from the campfire ashes. Somewhere from the tangle of forest came the pure notes of a bell-bird, and it seemed to Stacey the perfect sound to pierce so profound a silence.

It was beautiful, homey, appealing. But it was not Hal's dream. No cabins, no tennis courts, no gym, although she could see, as she parked her car, what looked like Alex's gymnasium equipment occupying a corner of the broad veranda. She thought of that rainy day in the pub when Hal had set out cutlery and dirty plates with boyish enthusiasm to demonstrate his plans. Her anger rocketed. 'Dad, how could you?'

She got out and slammed the car door, and its sound was sharp and shocking in that silence. She took her suitcase from the boot, then slammed the lid down. The man coming around the side of the house, arms loaded with cut logs, stopped at the noise. It was Hal, wearing a broad-brimmed hat. He stared, frowned, then came forward and looked her over, from her cotton trousers and oversized T-shirt to her hair, caught up in a ponytail. Then his eyes narrowed on her suitcase.

'You should have booked ahead,' he said. 'We're full up tonight.'

'I know all about it, Hal,' she said steadily. 'Dad shouldn't have done that to you. I should have guessed he might. He hates losing anything—deals, takeover bids, property, daughters.' She grimaced. 'He was bound to look for a scapegoat. I'm sorry it was you.' She looked around at all the spaces where his resort buildings should be. 'It must have hurt.'

'That's life,' he said drily. Seen over the logs he held, his face was only fractionally softer than the wood. Stacey wondered why he looked so harsh, so unwelcoming—quite a change from his attitude when he'd visited her place. He walked on towards the blackened campfire site. Stacey followed. The hat was an Akubra. With Hal's straight nose and his big chin it looked workmanlike but dashing. He wore a faded red shirt that stretched to tearing point across his back as he handled the heavy logs. His denims were the washed-out colour of the sky on a blistering hot day—pale whitish-blue. They hugged his behind and his thighs, and faithfully recorded every muscle move. The female guests really got their money's worth, she thought, studying him and getting hers.

'I could help you, Hal,' she offered.

'Thanks, but no, thanks. Let a Jamieson too close and all hell breaks loose.'

Stacey bit back her impatience. 'I could do a deal with Dad—refuse to tell him where I am until he gives you an introduction to a bank or a——'

'Forget it, Stacey.'

'Or I could——' She stopped as Hal rose suddenly close to her and put his hands on his hips. Brown eyes cold as cold black coffee, she thought. No sugar.

'Don't—you—*dare*—offer me money,' he said in a soft, deadly tone.

Stacey bristled. He didn't think she'd changed at all really, did he? Aping his stance, she glared up at him. 'I don't have any money to offer,' she said sarcastically. 'None I can lay my hands on, anyway, except for my savings for the past eighteen months, which amount to about six hundred dollars.'

He gave a short laugh. 'So you *did* get taken for a ride when you sold your car and jewellery!'

He'd hit a weak spot there. Months after she'd sold both, she realised she'd been short-changed. She flushed. 'None of your business. Anyway, I'm not offering you money, I'm offering you *me*.' She batted herself on the chest as she said it.

Hal's eyes followed the gesture. Tipping back his hat, he paced away to the nearest tree and leaned his shoulder against it, crossing his arms over his chest. The sun stippled his hat, gilded the hairs on his muscular forearms. The hat brim shaded his eyes, but Stacey could tell he was looking her over. 'Well,' he drawled, 'that certainly would be a great—consolation. But I doubt it would help Cedar Hill's profits.'

'I meant—to work for you,' she said, gritting her teeth.

'I don't need a photographer right now.'

'Doing whatever is necessary. Grace can't cook or do any lifting for a few weeks. You need someone to stand in for her. She needs someone around to keep her spirits up, another woman preferably, and one she won't resent too much in her kitchen.'

His mouth compressed. 'No, thanks.'

The fine leash on Stacey's temper broke. 'Oh, for heaven's sake, you and Alex can't do everything! And while I'm sure the ladies might be prepared to get by on that sexy Marlboro Man pose of yours and bread and cheese, the men won't.'

Hal broke the Marlboro Man pose and strode over to take her arm and propel her towards her car.

'I want to help you—what's the matter with you? I don't want wages, just my keep, until Grace is up and about again. Oh, I suppose it's your pride that won't let me—ow!' Stacey stumbled over a stone and he steadied her strongly. So strongly that she was close to him, the brim of his hat touching her hair. Her hands were flat on his chest, and he was warm with his own warmth and the sun's. The photographs she had of him, the beach candids and those taken in the garden that morning while he'd practised karate moves, were superb but not a patch on the real thing. They didn't show, for instance, the lighter gold-brown around his pupils, they only hinted at the wonderful asymmetry of his mouth. Stacey stared at it now, entranced by its slight movement, remembering how surprisingly tender it could be, how savage and passionate. She swallowed, and saw a similar movement in Hal's throat.

'I've got a business to run, Stacey,' he told her. 'Your father's interference has made that hard, but by no means impossible. I intend to have what I want eventually, in spite of him, but right now I can't afford to let Cedar Hill become the meat in the sandwich while you prove to him what a big girl you are now. And besides——' His hands slid down her arms a little way, then he let go and opened the back door of her car, slinging her suitcase in.

'Hey!' She was swung around again and deposited on the driver's seat. Hal leaned in, barring the door.

'And besides, what?' she demanded.

'You're too damned pushy!' he growled, then he bent and kissed her hard on the mouth, hauling himself back almost immediately.

Stacey licked her lips, confused by his attitude, encouraged by that impulsive kiss. 'Couldn't I at least have a cup of coffee before I go?' she breathed.

The effect of her words on him was galvanic. 'Coffee?' he echoed, his eyes snapping wide open in horror.

'Tea, then,' she amended hastily. He clapped a hand to his forehead. 'Hal, what's the matter?'

As far as she could make out, his reply was 'Aaaagh!' followed by some pretty steamy muttered curses as he hung on to his hat and took off across the shaggy lawn to the house.

Alarmed, Stacey followed him. 'What?' she yelled, her head swinging wildly this way and that as she looked for a telltale spiral of smoke, a snake, some sign of catastrophe, but all she saw as she tore in his wake was serenity. Watercolour paintings on pale walls, a piano and a big fireplace with more cut logs beside it and wrinkled sofas and fat armchairs. There was a glimpse of a corridor closed off and marked 'Private', and then the kitchen. Hal grabbed a pot-holder and pulled the oven door open. Cursing fluently, he withdrew a tray and tossed it on to the bleached kitchen table. On it were two dozen very flat, very black scones.

'Afternoon tea,' he scowled.

Stacey bit her lip at his glowering face; it was nearly as black as the scones. Washing her hands at the sink, she began opening cupboards. Grace had her system for storing things, and it hadn't changed. Stacey found flour and sugar, took milk and eggs from the fridge. 'How long have we got?' she asked.

Hal narrowed his eyes at her. 'Fifteen minutes.'

Fifteen minutes later Hal rang the bell and eight people appeared like magic from the forest and the tents. There were flapjacks and jam and cream for afternoon tea, a tribute to teamwork. There were three children among the guests, and their treble jammy cries for more were profoundly satisfying. Fifteen minutes after the bell had sounded, the big pots of tea and coffee were empty, the flapjacks gone, the cream dented with tiny fingermarks and the tables vacated.

Stacey helped clear away the debris, took it into the kitchen and turned triumphantly to Hal.

'OK, you don't have to fish for compliments,' he said grudgingly. 'The flapjacks were good. Thanks for helping out.'

'I never fish for compliments!' she protested.

'That's not the way I remember it. You were about as subtle as a steam train.'

Oh, yes, Stacey remembered. She had longed to hear him say he thought her good to look at, talented, that he found her interesting as a woman. What a single-minded, selfish little brat she'd been, provoking and teasing him when his circumstances made it impossible for him to walk away. And, being only human, he'd given her the response she'd sought once or twice. That night in the motel, for instance. Stacey had thought of that a lot since, wanting to believe Hal's lovemaking had sprung from his feelings for her. But with maturity she had to admit that the circumstances would have tried any red-blooded man. There she'd been, ripping her clothes and cavorting around half-naked, mock-crying rape. It had practically been an invitation, one she couldn't blame him for taking up. Oh, he had some tenderness for her, she knew that by the way he'd touched her and exercised a control that most men would have felt justified in throwing to the winds. But it was no more than that.

She slanted a look at him as she washed the dishes. It was hardly any wonder he was chary of accepting her help. Pride, of course, but maybe apprehension, too, that he would be lumbered again with the spoiled brat who made it so obvious she fancied him. Perhaps he thought she would continue the chase and embarrass him in front of his guests. Stacey ducked her head, embarrassed herself at the idea. 'You're too damned pushy,' he'd said just a little while ago. Oh, lord, her longing must still be showing. But he'd kissed her, hadn't he? Stacey considered that for a few moments and dismissed it. It was more of a rebuke than anything. It was only her own feelings for Hal that had made it seem so significant. He liked her, she wasn't mistaken about that. But she came on too strong, which accounted for his defensive manner. You idiot, Stacey, haven't you learnt anything in the past year and a half?

'Hal,' she said, concentrating on the dishes, 'I'm serious. I would like to stay to help out at least until Grace is fit again. My father won't know about it. Contrary to what you might think, I'm not going to tell him I'm working for you just to punish him. So you needn't fear bringing his wrath down on your head again.' He didn't answer. 'Besides, I owe it to you,' she went on. 'You saved me from scarring and maybe worse. You know how it feels to be obligated to someone. So will you please allow me to repay you in this small way?'

He wiped the plates and set them on the table.

'Obligated?' he repeated. 'Is that why you came here, because you're obligated?'

Yes, but also because I love you, you big ox, and it hurts me to see you working so hard just to keep the promise of your dream alive. She turned to look seriously at him. 'I feel at least partly responsible for the way Dad has victimised you.'

The dried plates went on to the shelf with a clatter.

'Well, don't. I don't want you obligated to me.'

'Too late,' she said with a shrug. 'I never properly understood the feeling when you talked about being in Dad's debt. I do now. It's ironic, isn't it—that I only met you because you owed Dad a favour, and now I owe you one?'

'You owe me nothing!' Hal spun her around. 'Nothing, do you hear?'

It seemed a repudiation even of the slight intimacy of creditor and debtor. 'What's the matter, Hal?' she flared. 'Is there only honour attached to paying *your* debts?'

He was silent, looking at her with that quiet ferociousness she remembered. 'I know why you don't want me around,' she said stiffly. He blinked a couple of times.

'Do you?'

Stacey turned back to the sink suds, making her voice light. 'Those bodyguard days must have been a trial for you. Of course, you knew I had a mad crush on you. It was inevitable, I suppose. I was immature for my age and you were a very attractive man. Well, you still are, of course, but you had more impact before when I was restless and dissatisfied with my life.' She threw him a grin that said, 'Wasn't it funny and ridiculous?' Or she hoped it did. 'I mean, you were just too good to be true, a real rugged hero type, with the mystique of a limp as well.' She turned to him and cocked her head to one side, lifting a sudsy finger near his cheekbone. 'Of course, a scar across here would have just made you the perfect mystery man, but I was pretty bowled over. The fact that you weren't interested in me was even more intriguing.' She grimaced. 'Most men found me and my money terribly exciting. Well, it shames me to admit it now, but I really did chase you in a way, and——' She ground to a halt, a bit put off by his thunderous frown. 'What I'm trying to say is—I've grown up since then, and you don't have to worry about a repeat performance.'

'That's comforting,' said Hal, as if he was sitting on a thorn. 'Who's your hero these days?'

'Oh, I've been out with a few interesting men. Paul and I see a bit of each other,' she said brightly. The truth could be such a lie. 'He's a teacher, but he's gone back to university to study psychology. You met him at the barbecue.' Paul had observed Hal and her reaction to him. 'The competition is tough,' he'd said wryly.

Hal gave a sort of non-committal grunt to cover his meeting with Paul.

'I thought it just as well to get it out in the open, so you know you're safe from embarrassment.' Stacey paused, but he didn't protest. Silly. She was half hoping he'd say he wasn't embarrassed and didn't want to be safe from her attentions. But Hal didn't utter platitudes and he didn't lie. She valued that, even if in doing so she had to bite the bullet.

'We were friends, Hal, weren't we? In spite of our differences and my crazy infatuation. We're still friends, I hope.' She looked around at him. 'Won't you accept help from a friend?'

Hal stared at her, but had no chance to answer, for Alex came in then, shedding a backpack, holding out his arms to Stacey. 'Girl, am I glad to see you! Saw your suitcase in your car. We really need you, Stacey. Wait till Grace knows you're going to stay on and help out!' He buffed her affectionately with his famous left. 'Isn't she a little beauty, Hal?'

Hal's muttered response was lost in the chatter of the other guests, who had returned from the bushwalk with Alex, and for the next ten minutes they were busy serving orange juice, iced water and soft drinks to the walkers. By this time it was four-thirty, and Alex was gearing up for dinner. After it was served he wanted to make a quick getaway to visit Grace in the hospital. Alex's assumption that she was staying buoyed Stacey up, but nevertheless, she hurried after Hal to get his final word on the subject.

'Am I staying, then?' she asked, hurrying along beside him as he strode into the nearest stand of box trees, dragging a sack behind him.

'All the accommodation is ful,' he told her.

'I brought a tent.'

'Then you'd better go pitch it,' he said, picking up firewood and tossing it into the bag.

Kerosene lanterns lit the veranda where the guests dined and the forest's insects came to worship at the yellow lights. For dinner there was fricasseed chicken and vegetables, and for dessert big wedges of Grace's apple pie from the frozen supply, served with dollops of cream from Cedar Hill's cows. Flushed from the heat of the kitchen, Stacey sent Alex on his way to visit his wife, and made tea and coffee in the big metal pots that had generous crocheted cosies that looked like Grace's work. Between them she and Hal set the tea things out on a table with cups and milk, cream and sugar. 'So much for the health farm diet,' she muttered, indicating the cream and sugar.

'Flexibility is all in this business,' said Hal.

While she washed up, Hal lit the campfire. It was dark by the time Stacey joined the twelve guests around the flames. And it was cool, for here, even this short distance south, autumn meant chilly nights and crisp mornings, even if the days were warm. There was no light quite like that of a fire on a cool, clear night, far away from city fluorescents and sodium streetlamps. It was warm and shifting, respectful of privacy and secrets. Beneath an electric light, faces had to tense to hide what had to be kept hidden. By firelight, faces could relax in the certainty that any secrets glimpsed would be too fleeting, too distorted by flicker and flame to give them away. So Stacey propped herself against a tree and watched Hal telling bush yarns and playing songs on the harmonica.

The plaintive notes drifted out across the stillness, joined by voices in songs old a generation ago. Hal might have had to postpone his dream, but he was making something work, she thought. Not a quitter, Hal. He'd weathered five months in hospital and a major career disappointment, and now he would weather this. Stacey joined in the singing, dredging up the words to old songs, and she smiled over at Hal, and in the deceptive flicker of firelight allowed herself the expression of love. And allowed herself to believe for a little while that she was reading what she wanted to read in Hal's eyes. But it was only firelight. Friends—that was what they were.

Hal's odd black mood passed as if it had never been. The guests came and went, and the number remained about the same, but the chores seemed to multiply. Stacey hauled wood and milked cows after several hasty lessons from Alex. She parcelled up tablecloths for the laundry pick-up, and when their fresh cloths failed to arrive, unparcelled them all and washed them, dried them, ironed them in a flat spin ready for the evening meal. She cooked, cleaned, watered the pot plants, then hit upon the idea of having the children cook a campfire breakfast for everyone one morning. Smoke-smudged, eyes stinging from the smoke which followed her wherever she moved, she led them in some children's songs while they prodded at sausages and bacon and constantly checked the billy boiling on the fire. Hal stopped by on his way to town for supplies, and grinned as Stacey dragged a smutty hand across her watering eyes. Strands of hair fell across her forehead and she blew upwards at them.

'How come you know so many children's songs?' he asked.

'Oh, my mother used to love to play the piano to me when I was little. She knew stacks of kids' songs. She really wanted more children, but she kept miscarrying.' She pulled a face at Hal's scepticism. Elegant Clare Jamieson, with her priorities of clothes and jewellery and her sense of occasion, seemed an unlikely thwarted mother. 'She had to fill her time somehow, I suppose.' Stacey lapsed into pensiveness. 'As their only child, I can understand why they didn't want to let me go. I just wish I could believe it was because they loved me too much. But I think—really loving someone is letting them go.' She turned to Hal, regarding him blearily through the smoke and tears.

'Yeah,' he said, walking away, 'but it's one hell of a risk.'

Grace left the hospital, and spent more and more of her time on the veranda rather than in the quarters she and Alex shared in the house's new extension. She kicked up a fuss about Stacey living in a tent, and Hal too suggested she should sleep in the house. But Stacey knew there was no room and refused to move. It was, to tell the truth, a pain in the neck sometimes, for it was the first time she had slept under canvas, except at school when it was done in style with hordes of other girls. She had borrowed the ancient tent from Liz, and it had been her first experience at erecting one. She had set it up a little distance from the guests, and she'd been pleased with it, even if Hal *had* come and bossily retied all her knots and criticised her site. 'Too close to the trees,' he'd said, looking up at the towering gums behind it.

'That's the whole idea,' she'd told him.

It was cramped, and she had to crouch to dress, but at night, when the wind blew in the trees and there was nothing to hear but the flap of canvas and the calls of night-birds, she loved it. Sometimes she got up in the early morning hours and walked around barefoot on the dew-wet grass, just for the joy of being the only person up. Walking was not always enough, and then she would fling out her arms and leap around in a silly little dance, or dive into the tent to take a camera from her weatherproof bag to photograph the false dawn and Hal's farmhouse where he was sleeping. But one morning when she twirled instead of taking pictures, he wasn't sleeping. In her nightgown and quilted windcheater, she twirled, in fact, right into his arms.

One minute she was alone, just the chill morning air rushing past her, and the next she was snuggled up to Hal's warmth, her hands clasped about his shoulders. It seemed so right that she didn't say anything at all for a while, just smiled. Then she said, 'Hello.'

He smiled back, his eyes drifting over her uncombed hair, her unmade-up face, her sensible warm jacket over her silly, silky, long nightgown. Her bare feet. 'You have this habit of running about at dawn without your shoes,' he murmured, and she laughed, recalling the morning she'd played her practical joke on him and found out the joke was on her. But then she bit her lip. 'Have you seen me—other mornings?' she asked, glancing at the house. Had he been at the window, watching her cavort?

'Not on purpose. I just always seem to be in the right place to catch your impromptu performances. Though your recent ones are much more circumspect.' Hal flipped the collar of her windcheater. 'A good thing too—this is a family place. Black lace and little red panties would earn Cedar Hill an "adults only" rating!'

Stacey was red in the face, and hoped he would think it the reflection of the dawn rather than her recollection of her unsuspecting strip, or her equally fiery reaction to being with him like this on an open stretch of rough grass with the sky streaked rose and the bush spangled with dew and the early-morning bird chorus rising.

'Monster, reminding me of that! I just may not milk your cows for you.'

'You call that milking?' scoffed Hal. 'You have to give them more than an affectionate squeeze to get enough milk for the morning tea.'

She was doleful. Milking was a chore she hadn't mastered. 'I'm getting better, though, aren't I?'

'Better and better,' he said softly. Then, in an abrupt change of tone, he said, 'There's a frost—your feet must be freezing. Put them on top of mine.'

'What?'

'I can't have a ranch-hand with frostbite. Stand on me—go on. Treading on my toes should be second nature to you by now.' Stacey did as he said and, with her bare feet planted on his boots, he walked across the wet grass to her tent.

Stacey giggled. 'This is crazy!'

'It's called "giant's steps". My dad used to let us ride on his feet when we were kids. He took such big steps, it was like hitching a ride with a giant.'

It was funny, but it was perilously close to intimacy. She had to stop her hands taking off on their own accord, had to stop herself swaying against him. Hitching a ride with a giant. 'Should I call you Daddy?' she laughed nervously.

Hal set her down at her tent.

'Please don't,' he said wryly.

CHAPTER NINE

THE GUESTS thinned out a bit, which took the pressure off. Grace still suffered blue moods, but recovered sufficiently to start ruling the kitchen again. Alex and Hal had time to work out, and the ca-chatter, ca-chatter of the punchball occasionally broke the sunny silence of a morning or competed with the drone of the lawnmower as the farmhouse grass was cut. On evenings when it was too windy for the campfire, they burned logs in the living-room fireplace, and the guests played chess or talked or just fire-gazed. Then, when there was room enough, Grace would sit with her crochet, while Alex and Hal played backgammon and Stacey knitted. The first time she appeared with her knitting bag they all gaped. Rather self-consciously she produced the twelve inches of cream wool fabric she'd made on her big wooden needles.

'Liz started me on it,' Stacey explained, a bit flushed. 'She's a keen craftswoman, spins her own wool. A friend of hers makes the knitting needles—see?' She showed the handcrafted needles. She was making a jumper for a friend, she said in response to Grace's questions, aware of Hal watching. He seemed intrigued with the image of her placidly knitting. Stacey was still a bit surprised at it herself. She'd started it with the need to prove that she could do it. Hal's certainty that she couldn't do anything so useful had rankled and, along with other glaring deficiencies in her life, knitting had become an important lack to remedy. Doggedly she'd set out to produce something, and she had in fact completed a jumper back

154

and was on the front. But now the urgency was gone and she was content to simply sit and discover what millions of others had done—that knitting was not merely a means to an end, but a pleasure in itself. The click, click of the needles, the pleasant pull of yarn through her fingers, the little rituals of turning, tumbling the ball of wool to release more thread, soothed her. It made her stop thinking about what she would do when she left here, made her stop thinking too much about Linda who, Alex had let drop, had come with friends and stayed here in her term break. Perhaps it didn't quite stop her thinking about Linda, who had knitted Hal the too tight blue jumper and who had looked as if she would gladly knit him a dozen more given half a chance.

'I was rushing to have this finished this winter,' she told Grace. The last week in June, she'd planned on finishing it. Two years exactly to the day she'd run Hal down in the drive of her parents' house and ruined his sweater. 'But now there's no hurry.' It was to have been her excuse to get in touch with him again, to give him at last a sweater to replace that damaged one, and as such she'd been anxious to finish it. Now, when she finished it, she would have run out of excuses to chase him up. With forlorn humour, she pictured herself knitting it for years and years so that she could hang on to her excuse to see him again.

'So it's serious, then, is it—you and this Paul?' Hal asked mockingly. 'Not just a onc-winter affair?'

Stacey almost laughed. How thick he could be! She was sure he would have guessed. She smiled and decided to keep it as a surprise.

'He must be crazy about you,' Hal said drily, eyes on the finished piece hanging over the edge of her knitting bag. 'You're a lousy knitter.'

Cheerfully, she agreed with him. 'It's the thought that counts,' she said, reminding him of his own words a long

time ago. Hal gave a huff of laughter that seemed to lack
real mirth. Then he turned back to the backgammon
board and received a sound thrashing from Alex. One
small mercy, Stacey thought as her needles clicked,
Linda's blue jumper must have worn out at last. She
hadn't seen it at all.

She took photographs, of course. The farmhouse
silhouetted against a purple afternoon haze, the rainforest,
the creek with its canoes and overhanging boughs and the
lush paddock of browsing cows, the guests, Hal himself,
his hat slanted over his face. Grace, restored to her
kitchen. Alex with the gloves on, sparring with a six-year-
old guest. Stacey contacted the local camera club and
inveigled the use of a darkroom, where she printed up her
rolls of film towards the end of her stay. They all looked at
the pictures in silence that evening, smiling, nodding as if
to say, Yes, that's Cedar Hill all right.

'You know, in a way, my father might have done you a
favour,' Stacey said cautiously. 'If you'd had the money
you might have pulled down or built over the best things
about this place.'

Hal nodded. 'It took me about three months to figure
that out. I've scrapped the original plans—at least for this
location. There's some adjoining acreage that would be
ideal for a health farm. But I'll keep this simple, countri-
fied, It's what people can't get any more.'

She was glad it wasn't to become sophisticated. Already
there were signs that Cedar Hill's simplicity and peace
would prove the focal point of the business. People
phoned to book, saying they'd heard about it from
friends. Hal had an advance booking by mail from an
American birdwatching club because they'd heard from a
friend about the wonderful birds in the forest.

But there was hard work to be done to keep the business
breaking even until it became established. The old house

was solid but needed care. The roof, for instance. It was watertight in rain showers, but might not be against a full-blooded storm. Hal started to limp, and that started him looking at the sky and the roof.

'Rain coming?' asked Stacey, pausing a moment beside him as she hauled boxes of fresh produce from the farm truck. Hal rubbed at his thigh, and gave her a quizzical look. His leg warned him of coming rain or trouble, he'd said.

'Well, it definitely isn't me,' she laughed. 'I'm no trouble any more.'

'There are different kinds of trouble,' he said, and dumped a box of lettuces in her arms. 'I'll have to nail down those loose sheets on the roof. The way my leg is aching, it can mean only one of two things—either a green-eyed, temperamental, spoiled rich brat is going to show up and run me down in a sports car—or there's going to be one hell of a storm.'

'Must be a storm,' said Stacey jauntily. 'That brat won't show up again. She's gone.'

Hal reached out and touched her face lightly, drawing his hand down to curve about her jaw. 'There are bits of her still around,' he said seriously. 'I was afraid the struggle might have knocked all the child out of her, but it didn't.'

'Child!' she exclaimed, trying to be indignant, trying not to lean towards him. It might be a 'just friends' exchange, but she could wish there wasn't a crate of lettuce between them. Wishing again. Hal abruptly withdrew and hoisted a sack of potatoes on to his back. He gave her a slap on the rump. 'Come on. I'm not paying you to stand about nattering.'

'You're not paying me at all,' she pointed out.

'Ah, but I'm feeding you, giving you a roof over your head.'

'I brought my own tent, remember.'

'Don't split hairs . . . the ground under your feet then . . .' he said mildly as they carted their loads to the kitchen and started back again, bickering, talking nonsense, laughing. Later Stacey climbed up on the roof to help him when she saw him wrestling with a loose sheet of roof iron, the wind, nails and a hammer.

'Get down off here before you break your neck!' Hal scowled when her head appeared over the guttering. She ignored him, clambered over and held the flapping iron down.

'Don't be so independent! I'll hold—you hammer,' she suggested, holding his gaze in challenge.

'Brat!' he growled. 'You still like to get your own way.'

'Sure. The difference is, I don't always get it now,' she grinned, and applied her weight to the loose panel. She was far, far from getting her own way. Being friends with Hal was wonderful, but she looked ahead and saw the problems with that. Friends sent each other Christmas cards and remembered birthdays and invited each other to their weddings. She didn't think she could be a guest at Hal's wedding.

'Finished,' said Hal, and the word struck coldly into her. She stood up too fast and didn't allow for the roof's slope. For a moment she teetered there, arms out like a tightrope-walker. Then, cursing fluently, Hal grabbed her wrist and she had a lifeline. In silence they stayed that way, arms extended. He held her strongly, and she steadied and knew she would have to let go of him and climb down alone. It sounded like a recipe for life, she thought, greedily recording this sight of him, his hair roughed up by the breeze, nothing but sky behind him. The mind took photographs, too. Stacey knew she would always recall this one with the kind of clarity that the day demanded. A day with a eucalyptus breeze and sun warming the roof beneath their feet and the clear call of a bell-bird. And loving Hal.

That afternoon, she took her camera and roamed about, making a last record of her stay here. As a friend she could come back again some time to help, or as a guest. But she probably wouldn't. Alex was in his corner of the veranda, working out with his punchbag and ball. Stacey took some pictures of him and lingered while he towelled off.

'Your stars say there's money troubles ahead,' he told her. She smiled. For Alex there had always been money troubles, she supposed, and her own these past eighteen months had certainly been educative, but if she wanted to claim it, her trust fund was waiting.

'I've got a million dollars, Alex, and the only trouble with that is ensuring you get the highest interest and the lowest tax.'

He danced about on the balls of his feet. 'Yeah, well, that's what they said. Money troubles.'

Dear Alex, as brown and whippy as ever. As devoted to his workouts. Still wishing he could have retired on his feet. 'I'm so sorry that man got away from you on the night of my birthday, Alex,' she said. 'It was your chance to get in that last punch and put things right, wasn't it?' His chance to hang up his gloves in glory. He looked a bit surprised that she understood that, but didn't deny it.

'Yeah, I messed that up all right.' He shook his head dolefully but recovered fast, shot out his left and buffed her gently on the chin with the brown, scuffed glove. 'But you never know, I might get another chance, eh?' He winked at her and went down into his fighter's crouch again, dancing, weaving, practising for chances that might never come. Some chances only happen once, Stacey thought desolately, yet what was there to do but go on practising?

Although the wind increased, the sky remained clear and the sunset was a glorious spectacle of lavender and tangerine, viewed by their current six guests over pre-dinner drinks on the veranda.

'I think you'd better sleep in the house tonight,' Hal said to Stacey. 'That tent of yours might blow away in a storm.'

'I'll be fine,' she told him as she tumbled a pile of Grace's legendary dinner rolls into a basket.

'You'll sleep inside.' His chin jutted formidably. 'If you're not up here by nine I'll come down and drag you out!'

'Caveman!' she mocked. 'How would that look to your guests?'

'Do as I say on this, Stacey,' he said, unamused.

So she slept on the living-room sofa until thunder and teeming rain woke her and she remembered she'd left her knitting in the tent. Would it get wet? Would it shrink if it did? Maybe that was what had happened to Linda's jumper, she thought, giggling, and got up, found a coat and a torch near the door and went out to rescue her knitting. The rain hurled down as if its purpose was to drive foolish humans into the ground. Stacey ploughed across the grass, dived into her tent, grabbed her knitting bag and dived out again, only to skid across the marshy grass. Her torch flipped from her hand and went out. As she paddled about blindly trying to find it she heard her name and called out, but her voice was neutralised by a mighty crack and a creaking, rushing sound that struck a chill deep into her. A great gust of wind swept at her, then came a deafening crash and the earth was shaking and so was she.

Shaking, shaking, she groped around and found twigs and leaves where there had been none—branches. Clutching her knitting, she got up, hearing her name again. Lightning flared and, sickly, she saw that she stood beside a tree. A tree, she thought. Not standing up, but lying down. She swallowed hard. Lying right across her tent. Someone came with a torch, and in its shifting light she saw Hal. The tree-trunk was almost as thick through as a telegraph pole, and he was tearing at its branches with his bare hands, bellowing something that was lost in thunder. The muscles of his back strained in Herculean effort as he tried to lift the log. Stacey swept rain from her eyes and gaped. The tree actually moved a few inches. 'Hal!' she shouted, as another guest's torch joined the first.

He whirled around, crouching, his hands held out and spread. In the pale beam his face was blanched, his eyes like those of a dazed wild animal. Still, so still he stood, brilliantly lit by a slash of lightning. She closed her eyes against the rain, and his frozen image was etched in negative on her retina.

Then he came for her, eyes never leaving her as he stumbled over branches and dripping leaves. His curses started deep down in him and grew like another storm building. He cursed her for pitching her tent near the trees, cursed himself for letting her. Cursed her for coming out in the storm.

'I came to get m-my knitting,' she stuttered. For a moment she thought he would hit her.

'Knitting? *Knitting?*' he bellowed, and picked her up, carried her to the veranda, and she could feel the depth of his limp and his pain. 'There's a shower attached to my bedroom,' he snapped. 'Use it and then go to bed. I have to check that the other tents are OK.' He disappeared into the rain.

Stacey showered and changed into the jeans and shirt she'd worn that day. All her other clothes were in the tent. And the tent was under the tree. The shaking came back. Grace appeared, woken by the thunder. Alex followed, wearing his old satin shaving coat with Alexander the Great in faded letters on the back. Stacey told them what had happened and broke into hysterical laughter. 'Money troubles, the stars said, Alex! I nearly got flattened by a gum tree and the stars predicted trouble with my cash flow!' Grace made some good, strong tea to combat the shock, but her intention to fuss similarly over Hal was firmly put down. He came in wet, glowering and limping badly. Taking a mug of tea, he told them all to get some sleep in a tone that brooked no argument, not even from Grace. Then he went into his bathroom and shut the door.

Alex and Grace went back to bed. Stacey filled a hot-water bottle and took it into Hal's bedroom. She turned on the electric heater. The room was big and old-fashioned, and so was the bed. She sat down and waited for him. The bathroom door opened and steam wisped out. Hal didn't see her at first. Eyes closed, he tied the belt of his towelling jacket and leaned against the doorpost, favouring his good leg. Face contorted, he rubbed at his thigh.

'You're in pain. Is it cramp?' she asked softly.

His head jerked up, his eyes narrowed on her.

'I can handle it.'

'You strained the muscles badly tonight. Have you taken pain-killers?' He gave a grunt of assent, winced and held his breath. 'I've filled a hot-water bottle. Lie down and I'll massage your leg.'

Heavily, he leaned against the door. 'Get the hell out of here, Stacey.'

She smiled faintly, copied his tone to remind him that the phrase was an old one. 'Not nearly enough conviction, sweetheart.'

A chuckle burst reluctantly from him. He'd always had trouble staying angry with her. When she went to him and put an arm around his waist, he looked down at her and accepted her help. Leaning on her, he hopped to the bed and collapsed on the edge. 'Leave it,' he said, stopping her as she made to push the robe aside. 'It's not a pretty sight.'

'I never expected you *would* have pretty thighs,' she told him, and again he gave a huff of laughter that wound up in a sharp intake of breath. 'Oh, for heaven's sake, stop being a hero, will you?' Stacey pushed past his hands and turned back the towelling robe. She swallowed hard, tears springing to her eyes as she saw the terrible scarring from his knee upwards. There were hollows where the flesh had never filled out again, and knots and ridges like denuded landscape features between the determined growth of sparse brown hair.

'I did warn you,' said Hal drily as she stared. 'Changed your mind about touching it?'

She blinked, looked levelly at him. 'Is there any oil in the bathroom?' He nodded and she went to fetch it. Hal stretched himself out on the bed, dragging a pillow beneath his head so that he could watch her. Stacey felt his eyes on her as she laid her hands on the terrible scars and began to massage the knotted muscles. Every now and then his head fell back and he gritted his teeth as a full-scale cramp hit. After a time the pain-killers took effect and he relaxed a little, closing his eyes. 'Turn over,' she said, and obediently he did, grunting a bit as she worked on the tight muscles at the back of his thigh.

The rain was steady, consistent, as if someone was conducting it to maintain the same density, the same tonal pitch on the iron roof. In Hal's room, lit only by the red glow of the electric heater, with the sound of rain and the smell of it, Stacey felt there was no more to the world than this—Hal exhausted and nearly sleeping while she eased his pain. He didn't open his eyes or demur when she slipped the robe down to massage the muscles of his back. For a moment she sat there admiring him. The sculptor who hadn't quite finished his face had fashioned his back into classic perfection. Squeezing out more oil, she placed her hands on him. This was for him, but it was for her, too. Opportunist, she accused herself. 'I half expected to see you emerge from the bathroom in a red leotard and blue tights,' she said, and felt his cough of surprised amusement.

'You think I'm a closet ballet dancer?'

'I thought you might have been Superman,' she smiled, taking pleasure in his small groans as she kneaded along the groove of his spine.

'Superman! I'm weak as a baby.' He smiled into his pillow.

'You must be Superman. You actually lifted that tree.'

'Everyone can be Superman,' he mumbled, 'if it's important enough. Read that somewhere . . . small man moves big boulder to free wife . . . mother lifts family car off only child . . . the power of love, you know.'

Stacey's hands slowed on his shoulders. She felt a little light-headed, a bit dry in the throat. 'Oh.'

'Had to lift the tree,' Hal rambled on. 'Thought you were under it.'

She knelt on the bed beside him. Hal's eyes flicked open and he, too, remained still for a long time while the rain came down and overspilled the gutterings in splashing, spluttering waterfalls. Slowly he turned on his side and looked at her kneeling there. He lifted a hand to her face and very seriously traced the line of her jaw, using the backs of his fingers.

'Well,' she croaked, 'that's what friends are for. To hold your hand when you're scared out of your wits and save you from plastic surgery and lift gum trees off you in a storm——' Her voice failed her—she couldn't sustain the flippancy. 'Are we friends, Hal?'

He nodded. His fingertips caressed her cheek, drifted

over her damp hair.

'Just friends?' She never had seen any reason not to ask what she wanted to know. Stacey thought she'd cured herself of the childish habit.

'It would be simpler,' he murmured, curving his hand to her nape. 'I was burning to see you again, and couldn't come up with an excuse until Grace went to hospital . . . but I only wanted to see you, make sure you were OK, find out if you'd found what you wanted. It was sheer luck you were having a party, because I had an excuse to dance with you, hold you one more time. But I wasn't going to get involved.'

'Is that why you looked as black as your scones when I turned up here?' she whispered. 'You didn't want me around?'

'Oh, I wanted you around all right. That's why I was so uptight. I wanted you around and I knew I was being a damned fool.'

Stacey uncurled from her kneeling position as Hal drew her head down to him, bracing herself with a hand on the bed, the other on his chest. This close, she saw the lines of fatigue around his eyes, the curling damp hair at his temples. 'I thought you were reluctant because I'd made it so obvious I was crazy about you before. That's why I said you didn't have to worry about a repeat performance.' Her progress down was halted. Hal looked in her eyes.

'This Paul——' he began. She shook her head.

'You're knitting him a sweater.'

'No.'

'Then who——' He stopped. 'Not for me?'

'Of course you, you big ox! I owe you a sweater, remember? It was going to be my excuse for coming to see you again.'

He smiled. 'Stacey Jamieson needs an excuse to do something she wants?'

'I have my pride too, you know. I was going to stop by and give it to you, make sure you were OK, find out if you'd found what you wanted——'

Hal laughed, wrapping his arm around her waist. 'Fancy that, the brat making me a sweater——' His face darkened suddenly and his fingers bit into her skin. 'You damned little idiot! You could have been in the tent when that tree fell, and all for some lousy knitting!'

'Not some lousy knitting,' she corrected. 'Your lousy sweater.'

He closed his eyes. 'Give me strength,' he muttered. Then, after a while, 'So—what's the situation now?' His voice was low and roughly tender.

'Well, I've done the back and nearly finished the front, and I figure the sleeves will take me about——'

His laughter shook him, vibrated through to her.

'I'm still crazy about you,' she whispered. 'Crazier about you.'

'And I'm involved,' he said, pulled her close. 'More involved. I love you, Stacey.'

'Hal—I love you so much.' She wound her arms about him and was content in his warmth and his love as they murmured silly things, asked lovers' questions and reminisced over those first weeks that would be the foundation of a lifetime's memories. The rain fell and the heater glowed red and Hal pulled the blankets up. In each other's arms, they slept.

The false dawn woke Stacey. The window framed the distant, rain-misted mountains. She turned to Hal, who slept with his head turned from her. His blue robe had come adrift in the night and hung over the bed on to the floor. He was splendidly naked, the bedclothes swathed around his hips. She admired him, desire warming in her. Last night they had been enchanted with each other in the new roles of acknowledged lovers. Last night their caresses had been loving, tender, heightened by a delicious anticipation. But there was no haste in them, and they'd fallen asleep instead of making love. They'd slept together. Stacey smiled, looked down at herself. She was fully dressed in jeans and shirt. She laughed softly, and Hal turned and curved his arm about her.

'What's funny?' he mumbled. She laughed again. His eyes were barely open and his jaw was rough with his overnight beard.

'I was just thinking how nice it is sleeping together,' she said, planting a kiss on his forehead. It was a much abused term, 'sleeping together'. There must be a lot of people who didn't realise the delight of actually sleeping all night with the one you loved. Hal pushed his other arm underneath her and rolled on his back, taking her with him. All the beautiful, naked length of him beneath her, and she had to be fully dressed!

'Nice?' he echoed, a gleam in his brown eyes. Hot coffee, with cream and sugar. 'Such a pallid word—nice.' His hands slid down her body, closed over her behind, gave her an erotic little jerk against him. Stacey's eyes flew wide open, and Hal grinned. 'Nice?'

She smiled, letting her body relax, letting the desire loose, yet relishing the wait. 'I love you,' she said huskily, and stroked the sandpapery texture of his jaw. Then she bent and kissed him, and he stayed still, letting her take the initiative, which was unbelievably exciting. First she kissed the downturned corner of his mouth and then the dented in side. 'I've always wanted to do that,' she whispered, slipping the tip of her tongue along his lower lip, teasing and pressing to get his response. He withheld it, and Stacey silently laughed at his game-playing. He might not respond with his lips, but he couldn't control everything so well. Breathing fast, she raised her head to look at him.

'Nice,' he provoked.

Stacey sat up then and unbuttoned her shirt. Hal hitched his pillow higher beneath his head, then crooked his arm under his head.

'Are you just going to watch?' she demanded.

'It's becoming a habit,' he murmured wickedly.

'Voyeur,' she said without heat, but she discarded the shirt and enjoyed the way he ogled her breasts. Dodging him, she got out of bed and unzipped her jeans. 'They're so noisy, jeans,' she complained, kicking them off. 'That night in the motel I must have taken five minutes to pull my jeans on because I was afraid of waking you.'

Hal's shoulders shook in silent laughter. 'Is that so?'

'You started rolling about and I had to freeze in case . . .' She stopped suddenly. Black lace and little red panties, he'd said when he found her twirling on the lawn outside one morning. Little red panties? He could only have seen them that night at the motel. Twice now he'd laughed like that when she mentioned the night—a secret kind of laugh. But if he *had* been awake . . . 'You let me go, didn't you?' she said in a hushed voice.

Hal's amusement died. 'You got away.'

Stacey shook her head. 'You let me go. You could have taken me back home and wiped out your obligation to Dad, but you let me go. That's why he was so vicious. He suspected as much. You must have given yourself away somehow.'

'Rubbish,' he scowled.

'You gave yourself away to me, too. I know you couldn't have been asleep. You mentioned the colour of my underwear.'

'OK,' he sighed, 'so I wasn't asleep. I had every intention of taking you back, but you hit a nerve when you said I was rationalising your chances of survival so I could satisfy my own need to repay my debt. You were so damned honest about how you felt that—I——' He shrugged.

'You did that for me? Hal, I——' She leaned over him, and was almost kissing him when she remembered. Her skin took fire. She shot up and threw a punch at his shoulder. 'You rotter! You lay there, pretending to be asleep, watching me tiptoe around, terrified I'd wake you——' Her colour deepened. She'd wiggled into her jeans, her bosom bouncing around. She'd stood like a statue naked to the waist because he was muttering in his sleep and might wake. 'You *pig!* You deliberately made me think you might wake up——'

Hal's shoulders shook again. 'It might have been my last look at you—be tolerant——' He raised his hands to ward off her blows. 'And I was punished. You took all my gear. I couldn't see what you were doing, couldn't believe it when I got up and found you'd taken the lot—ouch!'

'*Twice* you've watched me strip, you—Peeping Tom!'

'Now, Stacey—the first time you stripped, but the second time you got dressed,' he protested, hunkering down in the bed as she pelted at him. Stacey was furious. She'd shimmied and jiggled, all for his benefit. Her gratitude underwent another weather change as other things occurred to her.

'Damn you!' she said bitterly, tears springing to her eyes. 'I drove away patting myself on the back for keeping cool, outsmarting you, and all the time you were just letting me do it! God, nothing had changed, had it? I was just a puppet still, the only difference was you were pulling the strings instead of Dad!' She whirled around to get off the bed, but Hal dragged her back.

'I didn't let you go,' he said very quietly, very seriously, looking in her eyes, 'I just didn't stop you from leaving. You were talented and warm, and you had the guts to make the break that thousands of girls in your position couldn't. You deserved your chance.'

Really loving someone is letting them go, she'd said to
Hal, about her father. Her father hadn't done that, but
Hal had. He'd let her go even if he was wrapping it up in
semantics. 'But it's risky,' he'd said.

'I might have fallen in love with someone else.'

He nodded. 'I couldn't see any chance for you and me,
but I admit it was hard to think of you with someone else
anyway. Dog-in-the-manger attitude. I worked on it.' He
loosened his hold on her wrists, ran the flat of his hands
over her back. 'Never quite got rid of it. I disliked that
Paul character the moment I saw the way he looked at
you.'

Stacey pushed herself away from him. This man made
her so vulnerable, yet he made her so strong. How odd it
was that for every reaction he roused in her he had the
antidote.

'If it's any consolation,' Hal murmured, 'it was abso-
lute torment for me that night. First on the lewd double
bed, you in a torn nightdress and one breast peeking at
me.' He curved a hand to her hip. 'Have you any idea
what it does to a man to see a beautiful, passionate girl he
loves wiggle into her underwear?' He moved closer,
cradled her rear in both hands. His voice dropped way
down. 'You have the most glorious behind——' Stacey set
her hands on his shoulders and looked down at him. Her
blood rushed through her veins, all her body rhythms
picked up, her nerves shrieked the news.

'I first noticed it when you were grovelling at my feet,
asking if I was a married man.'

'I never grovel,' she said.

'Instead of censure I should get a medal for keeping my
cool when you pulled your jeans on and set everything in
motion . . .' His breathing was quite irregular. Softly he
stroked her breasts, raised himself to taste them. 'Ah, my
darling girl, I thought I might never see you again—might

never make love to you the way I wanted to that night . . . you left me in pain, truly.'

'Good,' she said, smiling, and lay down with him to marvel at the tenderness and the strength of his big body, the gentleness and the passion of his hands and mouth as he loved her, the almost awesome power of him as he came into her, his patience, his sensitive matching to her rhythm until there was no need for conscious thought for each other's needs, for they were the same. The same. She would always love the sound of rain.

Later, Hal looked at her as she nestled in his arms.

'Well?' he said softly.

'Definitely Superman.'

He chuckled. 'The power of love, sweetheart.'

They walked in the rain before breakfast. Stacey wore Grace's gumboots and Hal's Akubra. It was a morning to dance, so she danced, twirling in the gumboots, treading on his toes. 'How I love you, Hal,' she laughed, turning her face up to be rained upon.

He caught her in his arms and kissed her. 'Ah, sweetheart, and I love you.'

There was something about the way he said it, some faint trace of regret that touched Stacey with doubt. They walked past Liz's tent pinned beneath the gum tree, holding a bit tighter to each other at the daylight view of near-tragedy. On they walked past the tall, straight trunks of brush box looming out of the mist.

'I'd like to ask you to marry me,' Hal said abruptly at last. 'But I need to have more than mortgages to offer you before I can do that.'

Stacey sent him a sizzling look. 'You're too modest, Superman,' she drawled in an attempt at humour. But a dead weight dragged at her. Humour was not going to help.

'Try to understand.'

She thought she did. It had always been there between them, a small problem between friends, a big one for lovers looking to a future together. 'Money troubles ahead,' Alex had said. She should have heeded the stars.

'I haven't touched my money since I left home,' she told Hal. 'I wouldn't have to touch it in the future.'

'But you have it. You're a wealthy woman, Stacey, and right now I've got nothing but debts. It's why I tried not to get involved with you—the gap is too great.'

'I don't care.'

'I do.'

So there it was—his pride again. In silence, they walked back to the house. She was leaving today. It seemed all wrong.

'I'll phone tonight,' he told her. 'If the bookings are light, I can come up to Brisbane next weekend.'

'Fine,' she said. 'I might have the front of your sweater finished by then. But you probably won't wear it. Lousy, you said it was, remember?'

'Lousy for Paul, perfect for me.'

'Hypocrite!'

Stacey drove away after breakfast, wondering just how much profit Hal's pride would demand before they could be together. A year's worth? Two? The rain set in again and she flicked on the wipers.

CHAPTER TEN

THAT night Stacey phoned her parents and gave them her address. Her mother wept. Her father said it was about time she put an end to this silly business, and when could they expect her home again? He was aggressive when she confronted him with his victimisation of Hal. 'How do you know about that? Has Stevens been whining to you about it? Is there something between you two—because if he thinks he'll ever get his hands on my money through you——'

How ironic, she thought. 'What's between Hal and me is our business,' she snapped. 'And you don't know him very well if you imagine he wants your money. It was Grace who told me, by the way—yes, Grace. She and Alex are working for Hal now at Cedar Hill. You're creating quite a little enclave of displaced persons, Dad. Hal wouldn't have told me anything. He's as stiff-necked with pride and every bit as stubborn as *you!*' She raised her voice over his interjections. 'I won't be coming home to live again, Dad, and I don't know when I'll get away from my work to visit you and Mother. But——' she heard the plea in her voice '—you could always come to visit me.' Brian Jamieson wouldn't do that, she knew. It would be a tacit acceptance of her independence for him to voluntarily walk into her life, instead of drawing her back into his. She cried in her bed that night, cursing the pride and stubbornness of the men she loved.

Quite unexpectedly, her mother visited. Clare Jamieson didn't know what to make of the shared, rambling old house, or of Stacey's hair, which lacked the care lavished on it so passionately by Ramón, or her clothes, which were casual and colourful and not very elegant. Nor was she quite ready to grasp that Stacey went to work at Marshall's every day, accepting whatever tasks came her way, as befitting a junior photographer.

'You make the coffee?' she exclaimed.

'Sweep the floor, order the stock, man the front counter, do the black and white negs—occasionally I'm let out to cover a wedding,' Stacey grinned. In fact, she had shown some of her transparencies of Cedar Hill to her boss, and he had agreed to sell one of them to a calendar customer. The photograph of the farmhouse, set against misty mauves and blues, would go out on hundreds of calendars with a small print caption: 'Historic farmhouse Cedar Hill, Uki via Murwillumbah, now a guesthouse.' Hal had given his permission, pleased with the indirect advertising. Wryly, Stacey wondered what else she could do to boost Hal's profits without denting his masculine pride.

'But you have the money to start your own studio,' her mother protested. 'You don't have to be an office junior for someone else.'

'I intend to have my own place, Mother,' Stacey said firmly. 'I'm just starting from the ground up.'

Clare remained dubious, but she was more than half-way to accepting that her little girl had grown up. 'Don't expect too much from your father, Stacey. He's very bitter.' It wasn't really news.

At the airport, Stacey hugged her tight. 'Thank you for coming, Mother. I missed you when I left—you can't imagine——'

'I think I can. We all have to get used to missing things at some time.' Clare detached herself with dignity, smoothed her perfect hair, adjusted her pearls. 'We compensate the best we can . . .' There were a few lines on her lovely face, a delicate looseness in the fine skin on her neck. Her mother was, after all, ageing. Stacey wondered if she would have noticed had she been at home for the past year and a half.

A month went by. Two months. She turned twenty-three, and her mother sent her French perfume. Grace made her a magnificent cake. Hal gave her an Akubra hat. 'An Akubra!' groaned Stacey. 'It's almost as hard to rhyme as lustres!' Hal drove up to Brisbane and stayed one weekend when Graham and Jenny went to visit his parents. Liz was resigned. 'Och, it's like living in lovers' lane,' she said, sitting at her spinning wheel. But she was good-natured. Graham and Jenny were engaged, and clearly Stacey and Hal were serious. She spun wool for the wall hangings they would receive as wedding presents. Drily, Stacey told her there was no hurry with hers.

Stacey visited Cedar Hill again, taking Liz's repaired tent with her for propriety's and Grace's sake. Hal slept in it with her, and she wished they could simply hide away there for ever. Nuzzling in to him before a Saturday dawn, she said as much. He sighed as he drew her to him. 'I want to be with you all the time too, but it isn't that simple.'

'I could move in with you,' she suggested. 'I could do some contract work for Marshall's and I could free-lance.'

Hal gave a cough of laughter. 'Move in with me—with Grace around? Can you imagine it?'

She giggled. 'We'd get dinner rolls like cannon shot.'

'Porridge like wallpaper glue. I don't think we could survive Grace's disapproval.'

Stacey wriggled against him, all her senses racing as he stroked and petted her. 'I love you so much,' she murmured sliding on top of him. A magnificent place to be—on top of him; a tantalising place to be, Hal aroused and not wearing a stitch. Her pulses raced in anticipation. She wound her legs about him. 'Why don't we just slip away and get married quietly? I need you, Hal——'

He gripped her arms and held her off. 'Don't be pushy! I haven't asked you yet, and you know why.' It was said lightly, even humorously, but there was an underlying steel that matched the sudden strength of his hold. Stacey was peeved. 'I haven't asked you'—the assertive male protecting his right to ask, insisting that it was she who must wait to be asked. Stacey considered that she had learned a great deal of patience since she'd left Sydney; she considered that she had been particularly understanding over Hal's proud refusal to offer her any less than he thought necessary. But her patience ran out as he chose this moment to flex his ego. She rolled away from him and grabbed her clothes.

'Yes, I know why, and I think it's stupid. Pigheaded and childish and—meaningless. You're only worried about what people will think!' She dragged a T-shirt over her head and pulled on a pair of cords.

Hal propped himself up on his elbows. 'You're beginning to sound like a spoiled brat again, a thwarted, spoiled brat,' he said, and there was amusement in his voice.

It sent Stacey's anger soaring. He knew she loved him, and even if it frustrated him to have to wait, he wasn't at all dubious about making her do so. Arrogant devil. Conceited clod! 'It's true, Hal—you think about it. You're worried sick that there'll be a few nudges and winks behind your back and people saying, "He's on a good wicket there, you know, she's loaded," or, "Played his cards right, the lucky dog." '

He didn't look nearly so amused. In fact, he looked as if he were carved from rock. Fully dressed now except for her shoes, Stacey looked down at him. Naked, he was the most beautiful man—even the raised, buckled scars on his thigh could not mar him in her eyes. Her body was still heated with anticipation. It was an ache low in her belly, and she wanted to fling herself down again and kiss him and say it didn't matter. If it took a year or two, or ten, she loved him and wanted him. But his brown eyes were unyielding, arrogant.

'I won't be owned by Jamieson money,' he said in a low voice.

It was as if he'd hit her. Her breath sucked in audibly and she thought he regretted the words, for he rose and reached for her. Stacey snatched up her bag and keys and backed away, out of the tent, and Hal came as far as the opening, using the flap to shield himself. Against a backdrop of trees and tangled undergrowth he looked like Adam, with his torso and legs revealed but his vitals covered. Adam with a tent flap instead of a fig-leaf. It was hysterical.

'Well, if you think I'm going to hang around waiting until the ratio of your money to mine is just right, you can forget it!' she flung at him, and marched off, barefoot, down the grassy slope to her car. He appeared too late, bare-chested, barefoot in unzippered jeans, as she drove away. So much for propriety and Grace's sensibilities!

How ironic. Because of her father's vindictiveness Hal had been unable to pursue the venture he'd planned that could have made him successful. And if he had at least the prospect of profits, perhaps his pride would be assuaged. In a way, her father was still running her life, Stacey thought as she gunned her Renault past the startled cows. But not for long.

She made a lot of phone calls when she got back to Brisbane. She phoned the airport and her mother and some other Sydney numbers, and she wrote out another advertisement to place with a magazine and newspaper on Monday. All the activity on the telephone might have been the reason she had no call from Hal. He wouldn't have been able to get through. Good. Serve him right. But when someone knocked at the front door at six that evening, she ran to answer it, laughing, sure it was Hal, come to make up.

It wasn't. It was her father. Stacey stood there, the laughter dying from her face, her mouth open. His hair was perhaps a bit greyer, the crease in his forehead seated in now and permanent, his big body impeccably suited as for business, even though it was Saturday evening.

'Dad!' she croaked. She held out a hand to him, but he made no move towards her.

He cleared his throat as if he was about to address a board meeting. 'I was up this way on business,' he said abruptly. 'Happened to be in the general district, so——'

He left it unfinished, which was uncharacteristic. Stacey felt his hurt, felt the effort this was for him. What a killer was pride.

He cleared his throat again, said aggressively, 'I thought I'd come by and see if you were living somewhere decent.'

She stepped back and gestured him in. Her voice seemed stuck in the back of her throat.

'Your mother said you were sharing with three others. I hope you're not involved with some drink and drugs crowd——' He came to a full stop at the sight of Liz sitting placidly at her spinning wheel. 'Hello there—och, you must be Dad,' she said with a swift appraisal of his face and figure. 'Stacey described you perfectly—I'm Liz.'

He looked a little uncertain at that, but shook her hand and made some small talk about her spinning and wool, then turned back to Stacey, his face set in sternest parental lines.

'Would you like to see my room?' Stacey led the way to her bedroom, and he walked around it, then stood a long time with his back to her, studying the montage of photographs with a thoroughness he had never afforded her work before. In the old days he would glance and smile and nod and say, 'That's beautiful, Stacey' or, 'What a clever girl you are, my pet!' But now he looked and looked as if he would find her in her pictures, and his shoulders were very stiff and his back very straight. Tears spilled on to her cheeks as she watched him. He wasn't such a very big man, not as big as she'd always thought.

The silence built up and he turned to her at last, and Stacey knew a moment of amazement that her father too could cry as he held out his arms to her and she ran into them.

Give a man a clear, crisp night with stars, give him a breeze and the eucalypt scent of the bush and a fire, and his mind just naturally turned to things past, to opportunities lost. Longings and wishes. Give a man a fire and a few old songs, and faces began appearing in the flames. One face, anyway. A face that laughed and telegraphed every thought. A face that glowed. Funny how he'd once thought that Stacey's glow was the work of hairdressers and beauticians. The moment he'd seen her again he'd known the glow was all hers. Hal took a break before he began the haunting Irish song, 'The Rose of Tralee'. It was a month since Stacey had driven away. He hadn't phoned her until the next day, and her Scottish friend had said she'd gone to Sydney. 'Her father came to visit last night and I think they've flown down together,' she'd said. Well, that was that.

His five guests sang with relish, finding the words to the old, old song as if they sprang from race memory. Maybe they did. There was a lot of the Irish in Australians. *'She was lovely and fair, as the rose of the summer, But 'twas not her beauty alone that won me——'*

The notes of his harmonica and the voices drifted with the campfire smoke. He could use some excuse to chase her up again. Or he could bury his pride and simply say, 'I love you, I need you. I don't give a damn if you're rich or poor.' Probably too late. Stacey hadn't come back to the house in Brisbane and she hadn't phoned. Perhaps the pull of her old life, her family, had been too great. Hal played and gazed into the fire and his mind turned to lost opportunities. '—*Oh, no, 'twas the truth in her eyes ever dawning, That made me love Mary, the Rose of Tralee.*'

The guests were yawning by eight-thirty, and retired to their tents. Hal went inside, doffed his hat and dropped on to a seat in the kitchen. Grace and Alex were drinking tea and reading the papers. There was an air of collusion about them. Hal smiled tiredly. 'No more schemes to "bring me out of myself", please. How about some tea?'

Grace poured him a cup and pushed several newspapers towards him. 'We picked up the week's papers in town this morning. You should have a look.'

'The stars say I should be aggressive to get what I want,' Alex said reflectively, closing one of the papers at the horoscopes.

'Stars? That rubbish?' snorted Grace.

'Oh, cripes, yes. I only read it for a laugh.'

Hal picked up his tea and idly turned a few pages. His hand jerked, he scalded his lips with the tea. Cursing, he set down the cup and grabbed the paper with both hands. Stacey was on page four. Stacey in denim trousers and jacket wearing the Akubra hat he'd given her.

'In It To Win It,' the accompanying text ran. 'It was no surprise when Stacey Jamieson won the television set in a raffle organised by a senior citizens association. Miss Jamieson bought 100,000 one-dollar tickets in the raffle, which was expected to net a profit of around eight hundred dollars and instead swelled association funds by more than a hundred times that. "I just walked up to her in the street and asked if she wanted to buy a ticket," veteran voluntary ticket-seller Ida Matthews said . . .'

Grace put another newspaper in his hand. Another photograph. Stacey in a tailored suit, still sporting the hat. 'Love and Money. Stacey Jamieson pictured here at an auction . . . today donated art and antique purchases to welfare organisations. She bought the works totalling around three hundred thousand dollars at auctions this week . . . will be re-auctioned to raise funds for the . . . Asked what had prompted her run of generosity this week, Miss Jamieson said she was in love. Miss Jamieson, becoming known around town for her hat and her open-handedness, will fly to the Gold Coast on Saturday to attend the children's fund "Gamble for Kids" night at Jupiter's Casino. "I expect to lose,' she said cheerfully . . . Long live love, Stacey Jamieson.''

Hal burst out laughing. 'The ratio of my money to hers! *That's* what she meant by not waiting around. If I couldn't make it fast enough, she'd lose it——' His laughter stopped. He laid out the two papers and studied them. 'It's stupid. She shouldn't have to do this. *I'm* stupid.'

'Now you're talking,' said Alex drily. 'You'll be going up the coast on Saturday, then, eh?'

Hal frowned. 'There are five guests. If anyone else turns up you won't be able to manage.'

Grace sniffed majestically. Alex danced on the balls of his feet. He thumbed at his nose in the classic fighter's twitch that always broke out when he was agitated or excited. Hal raised both hands in surrender.

'I'll go, champ. I'll go!'

The casino tables were full. The socialites were there, the showbiz personalities. Old money looking bored, new money looking alert in the way new money had. Brian and Clare Jamieson were there, of course, for this was Clare's favourite charity and she was a member of the children's fund organising committee. The evening clothes ranged from artistic tatters to backless elegance. Dinner-jackets, dark and pale blue and burgundy. Two showbiz men had sequinned lapels and waistcoats.

Stacey wore a close-fitting strapless gown in green. Diamonds at her throat, high-heeled evening shoes—and her Akubra hat slanted across her forehead. The eccentric Miss Stacey Jamieson. She indicated that she wanted a third card from the dealer and turned up her other two. Too high. She lost again. She was really losing wonderfully well. So well, in fact, that quite a crowd had gathered around the table to watch. With apparent recklessness she bet another pile of chips and beckoned an attendant to get some more for her. She flipped a roll of money to him, and there was an amused little gasp from the onlookers and speculation as to how much more money she might be willing to lose. After her exploits earlier in the week, her father had asked her that question, his shrewd eyes assessing, calculating as he looked for loopholes. They might be reconciled and he might be wary of this daughter who now had some of his own toughness, bred of the need to fend for herself, but he still hoped for a return to the fold. 'I'm prepared to lose all of it,' she told him. 'Hal doesn't want to marry a wealthy woman.'

He found that hard to fathom, had to wrestle with his ingrained notions of fortune-hunters and opportunists and reach back to his own youth and to moneyless pride and dignity. 'He means that much to you?'

'He means everything,' she said simply.

He wrestled with that, too, for a while. Then he grew indignant that a man his little girl wanted would not co-operate. 'Doesn't he see that you're a damned prize—with or without money? The man's a fool!'

'The man's stubborn and proud and arrogant and pig-headed and I love him,' Stacey told him.

Her father seemed to find the description more and

more to his liking. Hal as a son-in-law began to take on a certain appeal. He was from a large family, which seemed to offer the chance of several grandchildren. He was a fine physical specimen, which also promised well in that area. He had the air of a successful man. 'Always stood out in a crowd,' he recalled. 'Yes. His own man, even when he was taking orders. Never anything subservient about Hal. Quite the opposite.' He talked himself into acceptance, from necessity, Stacey thought. Brian Jamieson could see she wouldn't be shifted, and he was the supreme pragmatist. But there was love there, too. He'd made the mistake of alienating her once, and he wasn't going to do it again. Hal would do very well, and Stacey saw him mentally lining up his future son-in-law in his sights.

'Don't do a thing, Dad,' she warned. 'No interference, please. Not even in his favour. Especially not in his favour. No moves behind the scenes to boost him along. Hal will do things his way—the same way you did when *you* started,' she added slyly.

She lost again. That made nearly two hundred thousand she'd thrown away already on roulette and blackjack, and there were hours to go yet. 'What's the bank?' she asked.

'One hundred thousand dollars, madam,' the banker told her. High stakes for high rollers and charity. 'Then I'll bet the limit—a hundred thousand. I'm on a lucky streak,' Stacey said beamingly to puzzled onlookers. An attendant came back with more chips and the news that her bodyguard was outside, demanding to be let in.

'Bodyguard?' she echoed, her eyes darting to her father who had joined the crowd around the baccarat table to watch her. She frowned at him, wondering if he'd reverted to his old ways, but he shook his head. Bodyguard? Stacey checked herself, then smiled. 'Please let him in.' She kept only two cards this time, a total of seven. Too low. She lost and placed another bet, her hands trembling a little, her heart thumping as she felt the shift of people behind her. She didn't have to hear his voice in her ear to know Hal was there.

'You don't need to do this,' he said, and her nervous system shouted out the headlines as she turned to look at him. Read all about it! Brown eyes the colour of hot black coffee. Strong coffee, no sugar. Roughcast sculptor's face. Hair recently cut. Shoulders big but elegant in dinner-jacket. Frilled shirt white against his tanned throat. He was going to look lovely in the cream sweater when she had finished it. She smiled at him, stroked a fingertip from his cheekbone down the grainy hollow beneath.

'You have the most fascinating face,' she said softly.

Hal was neither amused nor flattered. 'You've made your point, sweetheart,' he said softly. 'Time to stop playing games.'

Stacey drew back a little. 'You think I'm playing games, Hal? Did you imagine I would just kick my heels and wait around until your bank balance equalled your pride and pigheadedness? *That* day might never come.' Without looking at her two face-down cards she refused another card from the dealer. She couldn't go wrong. She lost and made a Gallic little '*c'est la vie*' gesture to the crowd. Hal's hand closed around her wrist. 'Give it up, Stacey,' he urged.

'No, no, I can't give it up now. I'm on a lucky streak— losing hand over fist.'

'I want to talk to you.'

'If you wait a little while I could be much poorer. You'd like that, wouldn't you?'

'Brat!' he muttered, and she thought for a moment he'd gone. But he'd only stepped back to improve his leverage. He turned her chair, then lifted her bodily from it. Her hat spun on to the table and someone passed it back to her as Hal carried her away. After the first startled reaction, people fell back at his approach. One or two men stirred as if they felt they should take some action on her behalf, but one look at Hal's face and the breadth of his shoulders appeared to dissuade them. A photographer snapped them. 'Is this the love interest you mentioned last week, Miss Jamieson?' Her smile was his answer.

Hal brushed past him and came face to face with Brian Jamieson. 'So. It looks like I'm stuck with you as a son-in-law,' the older man said bluntly. 'Promise me you won't call me Dad.'

'Promise me you'll cut your daughter out of your will.'

Brian Jamieson smiled. 'It's early days yet. I've given up smoking and the opera. I could live to be a hundred.'

'That might be a mixed blessing,' said Hal, eyes narrowed.

The two men eyed each other and appeared to come to some unspoken agreement. They each gave a tiny nod, and Stacey sighed at this exclusive male communication. She caught her mother's eye and waved the Akubra hat. As a member of the planning committee, Clare Jamieson closed her eyes briefly. As a mother, she opened them again and threw a little kiss at her daughter as she was carried off.

'A good thing you're taking me away,' Stacey said, hooking her arms around Hal's neck and kissing him. 'I might have started winning. And in my case, winning would have been losing.'

'Will you marry me?' he said, striding out into a palm-filled foyer.

'What about my money? I've given a lot away on the quiet, but there's still some left, I'm afraid.'

'I'll just have to hack it, won't I? You're more important to me than money.'

'We're in agreement, then. You're more important to *me* than money. This was the only way I could think of to show you——'

'Yes, yes, But will you marry me?'

'When you're successful, you know people will probably say it's because you've got a rich father-in-law,' she reminded him.

'I'll just have to hack that too, won't I?'

'But Dad won't interfere, not now. Not even to help you behind the scenes. When you get what you want, you'll have done it all by yourself.'

'Sweetheart, I know all that. Stop waffling and say "Yes, Hal", just for the record. Will you marry me?'

'Yes, Hal,' she said meekly. He gave a wry laugh as he carried her past startled patrons.

'It sounds good. I dare say I'll never hear you say it again.'

Stacey held on to her hat and him. 'Oh, I don't know. It's just a matter of asking the right questions.'

Hal's mouth twitched. He paused by the reception desk, where the staff tried to look professionally unfazed.

'The right questions. Hmm. If I could book a room here tonight, would you be interested?'

'Yes, Hal,' she said, laughter bubbling up inside her.

'Would you like to make love?'

'Yes, Hal.'

'I'm getting the hang of this,' he murmured. 'Would you like to——' He leaned close and whispered in her ear.

'*Yes,* Hal!' she said.

They were married in the gardens of Jamieson House. Mr Jaswinsky's hedges were smooth as moss, the lawns emerald velour and the camellias bloomed. It was a small wedding, much smaller than the one Brian and Clare had always had in mind for their only daughter. But they had reached this compromise to share the day. Grace and Alex came, putting aside their awkwardness at returning to the place where they had once belonged, letting go of any remaining bitterness for the sake of Hal and Stacey. Liz and Jenny and Graham were there too, gazing around in astonishment as they tried to relate the flatmate who had scrimped for her share of the rent with this luxury. Hal's family, too, had to come to terms with the wealthy in-laws to whom they had once owed a great debt. But the debt had been repaid, and they disguised their discomfort, welcomed Stacey with the generosity of a large family and met the efforts of their hosts half-way, and another compromise was reached. It was not the most comfortable group of guests, but everyone tried. Maybe it was a good omen, Stacey thought, to start off a marriage with so much give and take.

'Your father really *is* a handsome devil,' Stacey smiled, but she hardly took her eyes off Hal. No one came close. They strolled inside. 'Something old.' She sighed, looking around at her old home. 'Something new.' She held out her left hand where her wedding band gleamed. Then she twirled so that her dress flared out to reveal a blue-trimmed underskirt. 'Something blue.' She smiled as she trod on his toes and ended up in his arms.

'What about the something borrowed?' murmured Hal, nuzzling into her neck. There was a delicate 'ahem', and they drew apart as the housekeeper informed Stacey that someone was asking to see her. 'His name is Connor, ma'am.'

'Mr Connor? Show him in.'

'Who is this Connor who has the nerve to call on our wedding day?' Hal wanted to know.

'I told him to. I advertised for him.'

'You advertised for a man? Now, why don't I like the sound of that?'

Mr Connor was in his late sixties and skinny, stooped forward as if he was permanently looking for something. He carried a small bag that was as worn as his suit, but not as worn as his face. Rather uncertainly he took in Hal's pale grey morning-suit, Stacey's wedding gown and veil. She smiled.

'We look as if we belong on top of a cake, don't we? I'm so pleased to meet you——'

Mr Connor looked a bit nonplussed. 'If this is incon- venient——'

'No, please.' Stacey beamed at him. 'Would you like a drink and some wedding cake?'

'Oh—that's nice, but—well, I don't want to rush you, but I've got a cab waiting. The meter's running,' he confided with a rather wry grimace.

'I understand. This way, Mr Connor.'

They went up the great staircase and along the gallery to Stacey's old room. Hal threw her a quizzical look and she smiled. 'Wait and see'. The room was basically unchanged but for a colour change to satisfy her mother's bi-annual decorating urges. Her furniture remained and the shells were still there. After years of urging Stacey to get rid of them, Clare hadn't been able to throw them out when Stacey was gone.

It was to the shells that Mr Connor headed. 'Well, well!' he kept saying, touching this one and that with careful fingers. 'My voluta imperialis,' he muttered. 'Found this with my mate Harry, poor old Harry—ah——' He picked up another and another, coming to each as if it was an old friend. 'Lambis rugosa,' he breathed, touching curved spikes. 'And my Star—I swapped a stromb for that . . . well. Well.' At length, he looked around at Stacey and Hal. 'You're sure? I can take them—I mean, you don't want anything for them?'

'They're yours,' said Stacey, going over to touch her favourites. 'They always were. I used to call them my jewels——' She smiled. 'I'm afraid one is missing. A little stray boy got to one of them before I could discover it.'

He hardly heard her. He was putting his shells in his

bag, which had dozens of little compartments. 'I didn't want to sell them, but things were bad and your father gave me a fair price.'

'Your wife was sick—did she recover?' asked Stacey.

'Yes, yes, she did. It'll please her that I've got these back again. She always felt a bit guilty, you know, that I had to sell them because of her.' He clipped up his bag, turned to Stacey and impulsively took her hand. 'Thank you. Thank you.' He shook Hal's hand, too, and hurried down to his waiting cab. Through the french doors they watched the taxi slide past the cypress trees.

'Something borrowed,' Stacey said softly, leaning back against Hal.

'You advertised to find him, so he coud have them back. You're quite a woman, Stacey Stevens.'

She laughed at the sound of her new name. 'I know. I've even started my new collection already, see?'

Hal looked. On top of the case was one shell Mr Connor had left. One she'd found while she walked on the sand with Hal. 'My first real "jewel in the sand".' It was a pretty shell with a few dominant stripes and a nice little curl on one side and a tiny hole to render it imperfect.

'I found it *all* by myself,' she said softly, linking her arms behind Hal's neck.

'So you did,' he said.